GOSCI~~NNY~~ ... ~~UDE~~RZO
PRESENT

# ASTERIX AND OBELIX'S BIRTHDAY
## The Golden Book

*October 1959. It's been all of half a century!*
*How time flies!*
*I remember my birth as if it were yesterday. My two fathers had decided that I would be born in the pages of a new magazine called «Pilote», which also contained stories about many other strip cartoon heroes. You could say the magazine was like a mother to us. And so I and the other Gauls happily enjoyed our adventures for eighteen marvellous years, until the day when one of our two fathers, the great René Goscinny, left us far too soon for the wonderful gardens of the Gaulish Paradise.*

*At that point, some people thought and said that Obelix and I and the rest of us were destined to join him there for all eternity. But after a very sad and difficult period our other father, the one whose drawings had already brought us to life, decided that he would go on working by himself to give us more adventures. It was you, dear readers, whose pleas encouraged him to embark on this dangerous venture. He had to believe in it, for as some charitable souls still think, it could have turned out an impossible task. Without his partner, people said, he could not succeed. However, he bet himself that he could — and won his bet. Our adventures are as successful as ever.*

*And so we discovered that those who may seem to be idiots have the great advantage of always believing in what they think, what they say and what they write . . .*

*Asterix*

Your voice echoes in my own, Asterix. Your ink runs in my veins, my blood runs in yours. And on this day our two voices conjure up a life — your life. You were born of the friendship between my father and Albert Uderzo. Each of them had his own talents, and they complemented one another. It was a perfect friendship, and it gave birth to a village and its inhabitants, dozens of wild boars, as well as Julius Caesar and his legions, who meet with unlikely resistance that sometimes leaves them battered and bruised. Above all, it was responsible for a great many smiles, a great deal of laughter, and a whole way of life for some people. Many people discovered the joys of reading, all because of the friendship between your two fathers.

However, you and I both have a debt to pay, Asterix. On a morning in November 1977, one of your fathers died. He was my own father. And you might have died as well, leaving a lasting trace on the memory of your readers, but no more. Rather as if I had stayed at the age of nine for ever. However, we were not alone. One of the two friends who created you was left, and I could hope that he would keep you alive, carrying on despite the nasty trick some evil genie had played on us. Fatherless at the age of nine, I said to myself, like a child reciting a nursery rhyme: "If Asterix survives, then I promise to think that death is a joke — a bad joke, but a joke all the same. I'll tell myself that imagination can win out over reality."

You lived, and so did I, thanks to the goodwill of the Orpheus who wouldn't accept what Fate had done to us. You had more sense than Orpheus, Asterix, you didn't turn round to look back, you looked straight ahead. And there was life ahead. You understood what really mattered: the story must go on.

On birthdays we celebrate the year that has just passed. We tell those we love something that they already know, though they may sometimes pretend to forget it: we tell them how important they are in our lives. Finally, on birthdays we look at the balance sheet of the four seasons that have passed. From winter snow to spring buds, we wonder, have we been worthy of our loved ones? So, Asterix, let me speak for your father and mine, and say I feel sure that, thanks to Albert Uderzo's talent, you will prove worthy of your Golden Jubilee, and that this book, with you at its centre, will show that you are as loyal to your readers as they are to you. If I had to say one thing about all the seasons that have passed, it would simply be: "Look ahead to the future."

Anne Goscinny

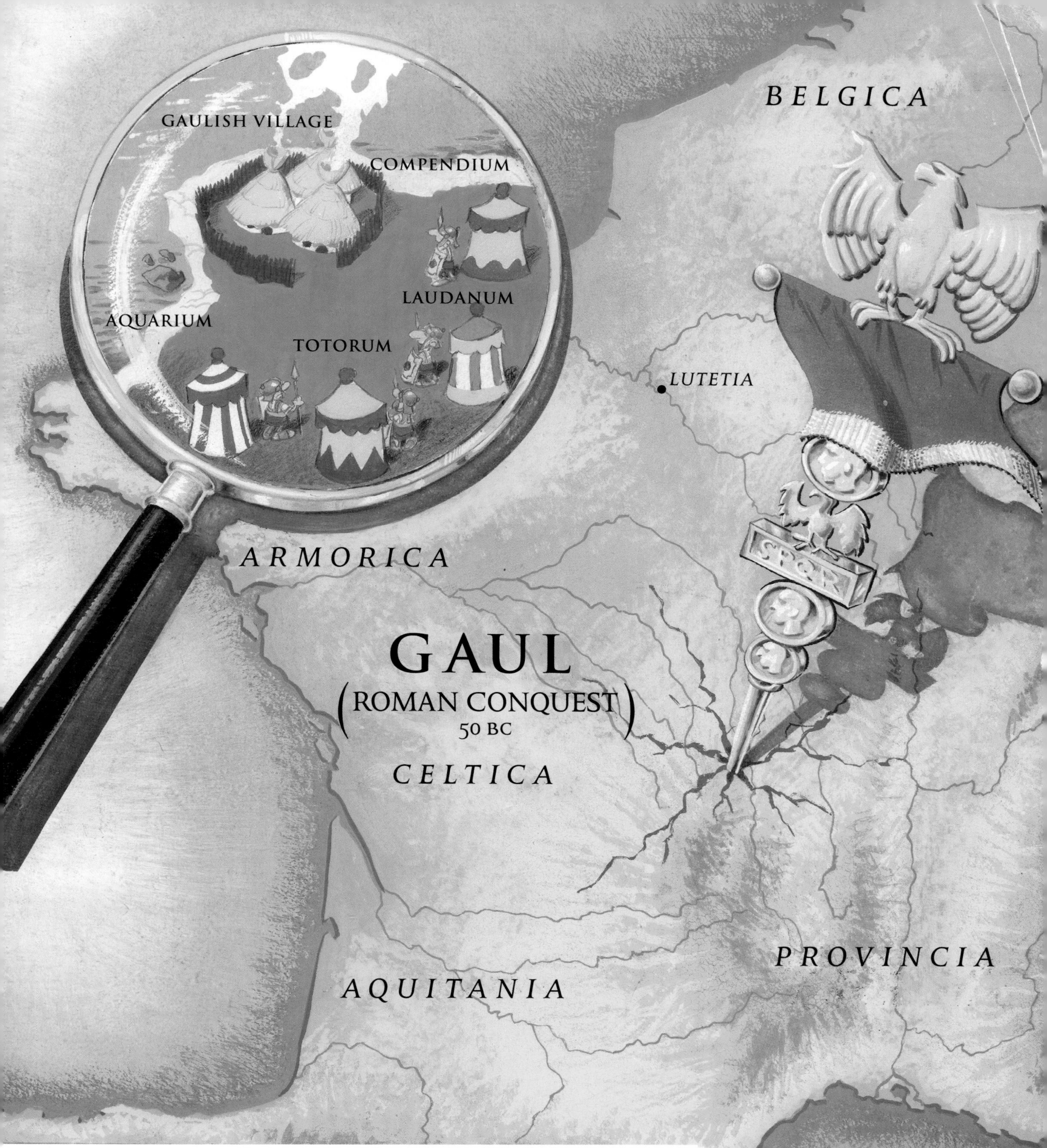
BELGICA
GAULISH VILLAGE
COMPENDIUM
LAUDANUM
AQUARIUM
TOTORUM
LUTETIA
SPQR
ARMORICA
GAUL
(ROMAN CONQUEST)
50 BC
CELTICA
PROVINCIA
AQUITANIA

THE YEAR IS 50 BC. GAUL IS ENTIRELY OCCUPIED BY THE ROMANS. WELL, NOT ENTIRELY ... ONE SMALL VILLAGE OF INDOMITABLE GAULS STILL HOLDS OUT AGAINST THE INVADERS. AND LIFE IS NOT EASY FOR THE ROMAN LEGIONARIES WHO GARRISON THE FORTIFIED CAMPS OF TOTORUM, AQUARIUM, LAUDANUM AND COMPENDIUM ...

ASTERIX, THE HERO OF THESE ADVENTURES. A SHREWD, CUNNING LITTLE WARRIOR, ALL PERILOUS MISSIONS ARE IMMEDIATELY ENTRUSTED TO HIM. ASTERIX GETS HIS SUPERHUMAN STRENGTH FROM THE MAGIC POTION BREWED BY THE DRUID GETAFIX . . .

OBELIX, ASTERIX'S INSEPARABLE FRIEND. A MENHIR DELIVERY MAN BY TRADE, ADDICTED TO WILD BOAR, OBELIX IS ALWAYS READY TO DROP EVERYTHING AND GO OFF ON A NEW ADVENTURE WITH ASTERIX – SO LONG AS THERE'S WILD BOAR TO EAT, AND PLENTY OF FIGHTING. HIS CONSTANT COMPANION IS DOGMATIX, THE ONLY KNOWN CANINE ECOLOGIST, WHO HOWLS WITH DESPAIR WHEN A TREE IS CUT DOWN.

GETAFIX, THE VENERABLE VILLAGE DRUID, GATHERS MISTLETOE AND BREWS MAGIC POTIONS. HIS SPECIALITY IS THE POTION WHICH GIVES THE DRINKER SUPERHUMAN STRENGTH. BUT GETAFIX ALSO HAS OTHER RECIPIES UP HIS SLEEVE . . .

CACOFONIX, THE BARD. OPINION IS DIVIDED AS TO HIS MUSICAL GIFTS. CACOFONIX THINKS HE'S A GENIUS. EVERY-ONE ELSE THINKS HE'S UNSPEAKABLE. BUT AS LONG AS HE DOESN'T SPEAK, LET ALONE SING, EVERYBODY LIKES HIM . . .

FINALLY, VITALSTATISTIX, THE CHIEF OF THE TRIBE. MAJESTIC, BRAVE AND HOT-TEMPERED, THE OLD WARRIOR IS RESPECTED BY HIS MEN AND FEARED BY HIS ENEMIES. VITALSTATISTIX HIMSELF HAS ONLY ONE FEAR, HE IS AFRAID THAT THE SKY MAY FALL ON HIS HEAD TOMORROW. BUT AS HE ALWAYS SAYS, TOMORROW NEVER COMES.

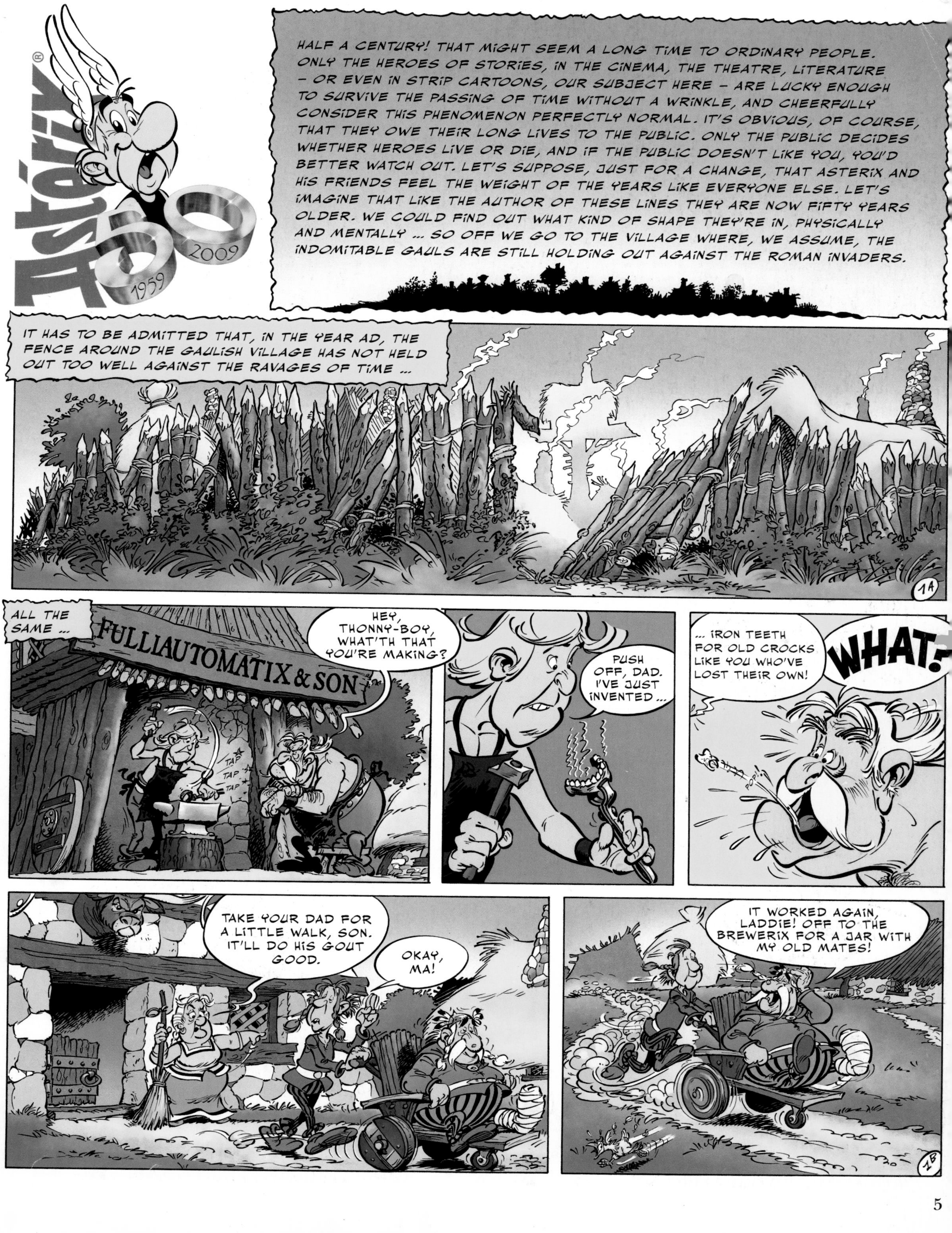

Asterix 50 1959 2009
HALF A CENTURY! THAT MIGHT SEEM A LONG TIME TO ORDINARY PEOPLE. ONLY THE HEROES OF STORIES, IN THE CINEMA, THE THEATRE, LITERATURE – OR EVEN IN STRIP CARTOONS, OUR SUBJECT HERE – ARE LUCKY ENOUGH TO SURVIVE THE PASSING OF TIME WITHOUT A WRINKLE, AND CHEERFULLY CONSIDER THIS PHENOMENON PERFECTLY NORMAL. IT'S OBVIOUS, OF COURSE, THAT THEY OWE THEIR LONG LIVES TO THE PUBLIC. ONLY THE PUBLIC DECIDES WHETHER HEROES LIVE OR DIE, AND IF THE PUBLIC DOESN'T LIKE YOU, YOU'D BETTER WATCH OUT. LET'S SUPPOSE, JUST FOR A CHANGE, THAT ASTERIX AND HIS FRIENDS FEEL THE WEIGHT OF THE YEARS LIKE EVERYONE ELSE. LET'S IMAGINE THAT LIKE THE AUTHOR OF THESE LINES THEY ARE NOW FIFTY YEARS OLDER. WE COULD FIND OUT WHAT KIND OF SHAPE THEY'RE IN, PHYSICALLY AND MENTALLY ... SO OFF WE GO TO THE VILLAGE WHERE, WE ASSUME, THE INDOMITABLE GAULS ARE STILL HOLDING OUT AGAINST THE ROMAN INVADERS.
IT HAS TO BE ADMITTED THAT, IN THE YEAR AD, THE FENCE AROUND THE GAULISH VILLAGE HAS NOT HELD OUT TOO WELL AGAINST THE RAVAGES OF TIME ...
1A
ALL THE SAME ...
FULLIAUTOMATIX & SON
TAP TAP TAP
HEY, THONNY-BOY, WHAT'TH THAT YOU'RE MAKING?
PUSH OFF, DAD. I'VE JUST INVENTED ...
... IRON TEETH FOR OLD CROCKS LIKE YOU WHO'VE LOST THEIR OWN!
WHAT!
POP!
TAKE YOUR DAD FOR A LITTLE WALK, SON. IT'LL DO HIS GOUT GOOD.
OKAY, MA!
IT WORKED AGAIN, LADDIE! OFF TO THE BREWERIX FOR A JAR WITH MY OLD MATES!
1B

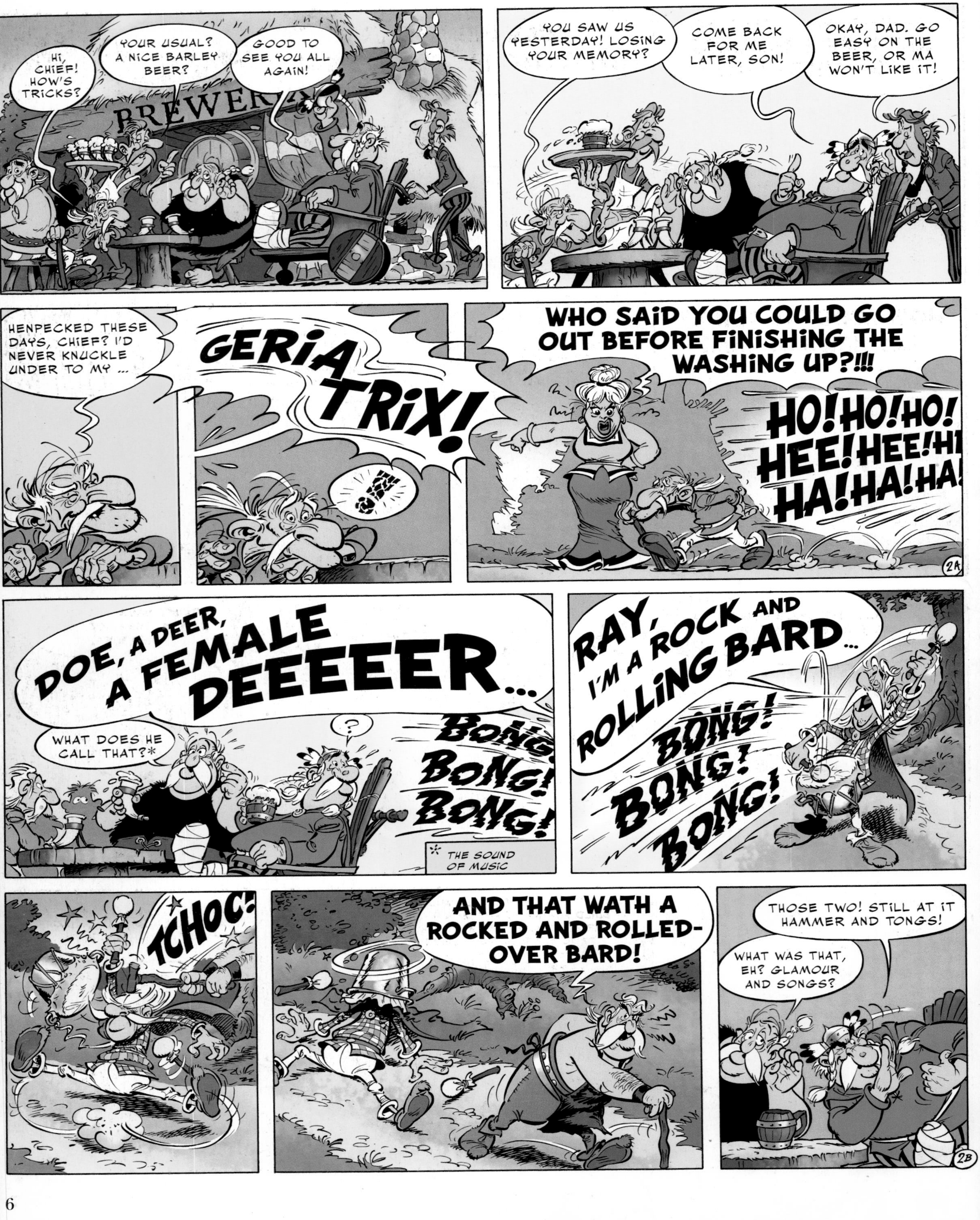
HI, CHIEF! HOW'S TRICKS?
YOUR USUAL? A NICE BARLEY BEER?
GOOD TO SEE YOU ALL AGAIN!
BREWERY
YOU SAW US YESTERDAY! LOSING YOUR MEMORY?
COME BACK FOR ME LATER, SON!
OKAY, DAD. GO EASY ON THE BEER, OR MA WON'T LIKE IT!
HENPECKED THESE DAYS, CHIEF? I'D NEVER KNUCKLE UNDER TO MY ...
GERIATRIX!
WHO SAID YOU COULD GO OUT BEFORE FINISHING THE WASHING UP?!!!
HO! HO! HO! HEE! HEE! HA! HA! HA!
2A
DOE, A DEER, A FEMALE DEEEEER...
WHAT DOES HE CALL THAT?*
?
BONG! BONG! BONG!
* THE SOUND OF MUSIC
RAY, I'M A ROCK AND ROLLING BARD...
BONG! BONG! BONG!
TCHOC!
AND THAT WATH A ROCKED AND ROLLED-OVER BARD!
THOSE TWO! STILL AT IT HAMMER AND TONGS!
WHAT WAS THAT, EH? GLAMOUR AND SONGS?
2B

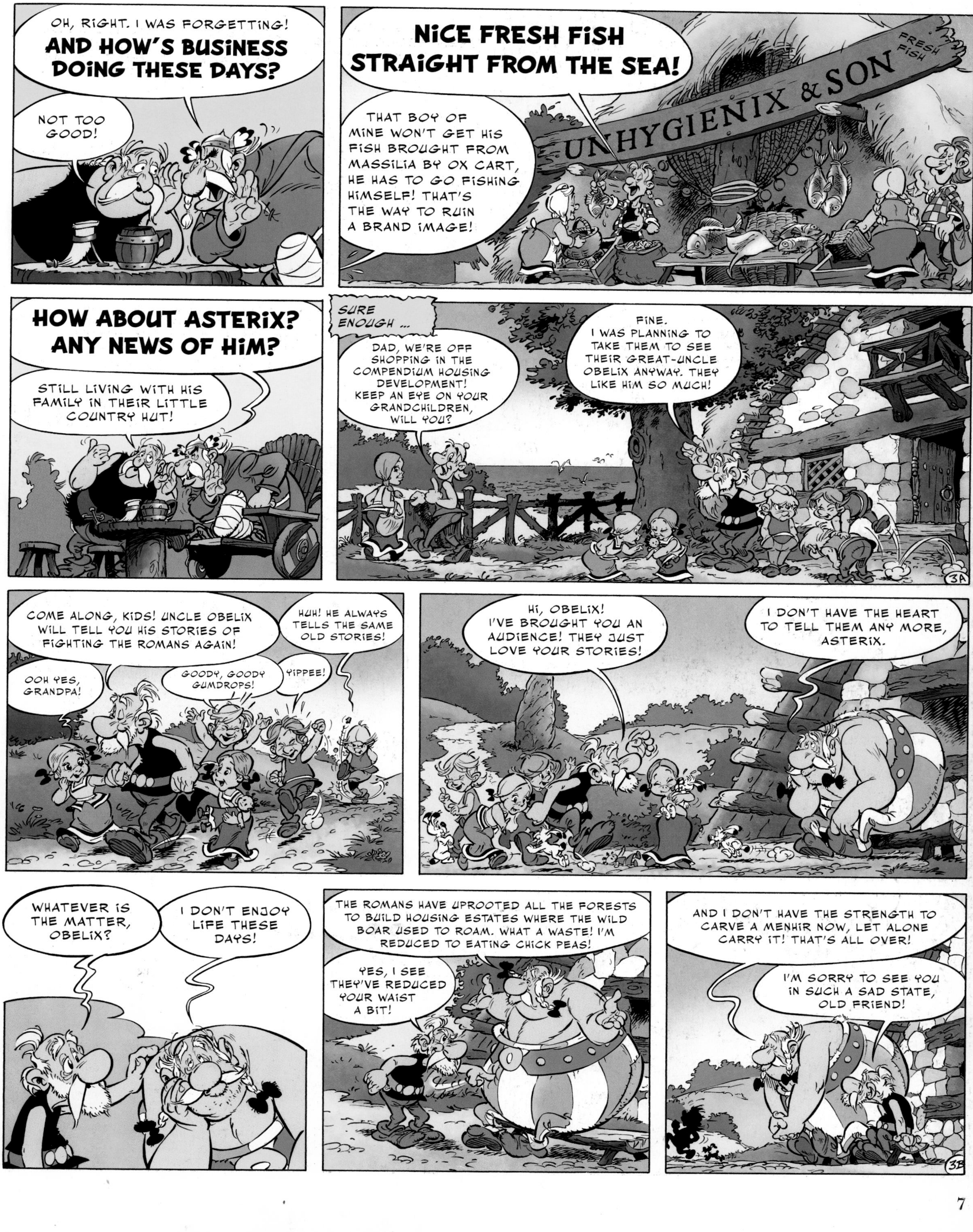

OH, RIGHT. I WAS FORGETTING! AND HOW'S BUSINESS DOING THESE DAYS?
NOT TOO GOOD!
NICE FRESH FISH STRAIGHT FROM THE SEA!
UNHYGIENIX & SON
FRESH FISH
THAT BOY OF MINE WON'T GET HIS FISH BROUGHT FROM MASSILIA BY OX CART, HE HAS TO GO FISHING HIMSELF! THAT'S THE WAY TO RUIN A BRAND IMAGE!
HOW ABOUT ASTERIX? ANY NEWS OF HIM?
STILL LIVING WITH HIS FAMILY IN THEIR LITTLE COUNTRY HUT!
SURE ENOUGH ...
DAD, WE'RE OFF SHOPPING IN THE COMPENDIUM HOUSING DEVELOPMENT! KEEP AN EYE ON YOUR GRANDCHILDREN, WILL YOU?
FINE. I WAS PLANNING TO TAKE THEM TO SEE THEIR GREAT-UNCLE OBELIX ANYWAY. THEY LIKE HIM SO MUCH!
3A
COME ALONG, KIDS! UNCLE OBELIX WILL TELL YOU HIS STORIES OF FIGHTING THE ROMANS AGAIN!
HUH! HE ALWAYS TELLS THE SAME OLD STORIES!
OOH YES, GRANDPA!
GOODY, GOODY GUMDROPS!
YIPPEE!
HI, OBELIX! I'VE BROUGHT YOU AN AUDIENCE! THEY JUST LOVE YOUR STORIES!
I DON'T HAVE THE HEART TO TELL THEM ANY MORE, ASTERIX.
WHATEVER IS THE MATTER, OBELIX?
I DON'T ENJOY LIFE THESE DAYS!
THE ROMANS HAVE UPROOTED ALL THE FORESTS TO BUILD HOUSING ESTATES WHERE THE WILD BOAR USED TO ROAM. WHAT A WASTE! I'M REDUCED TO EATING CHICK PEAS!
YES, I SEE THEY'VE REDUCED YOUR WAIST A BIT!
AND I DON'T HAVE THE STRENGTH TO CARVE A MENHIR NOW, LET ALONE CARRY IT! THAT'S ALL OVER!
I'M SORRY TO SEE YOU IN SUCH A SAD STATE, OLD FRIEND!
3B

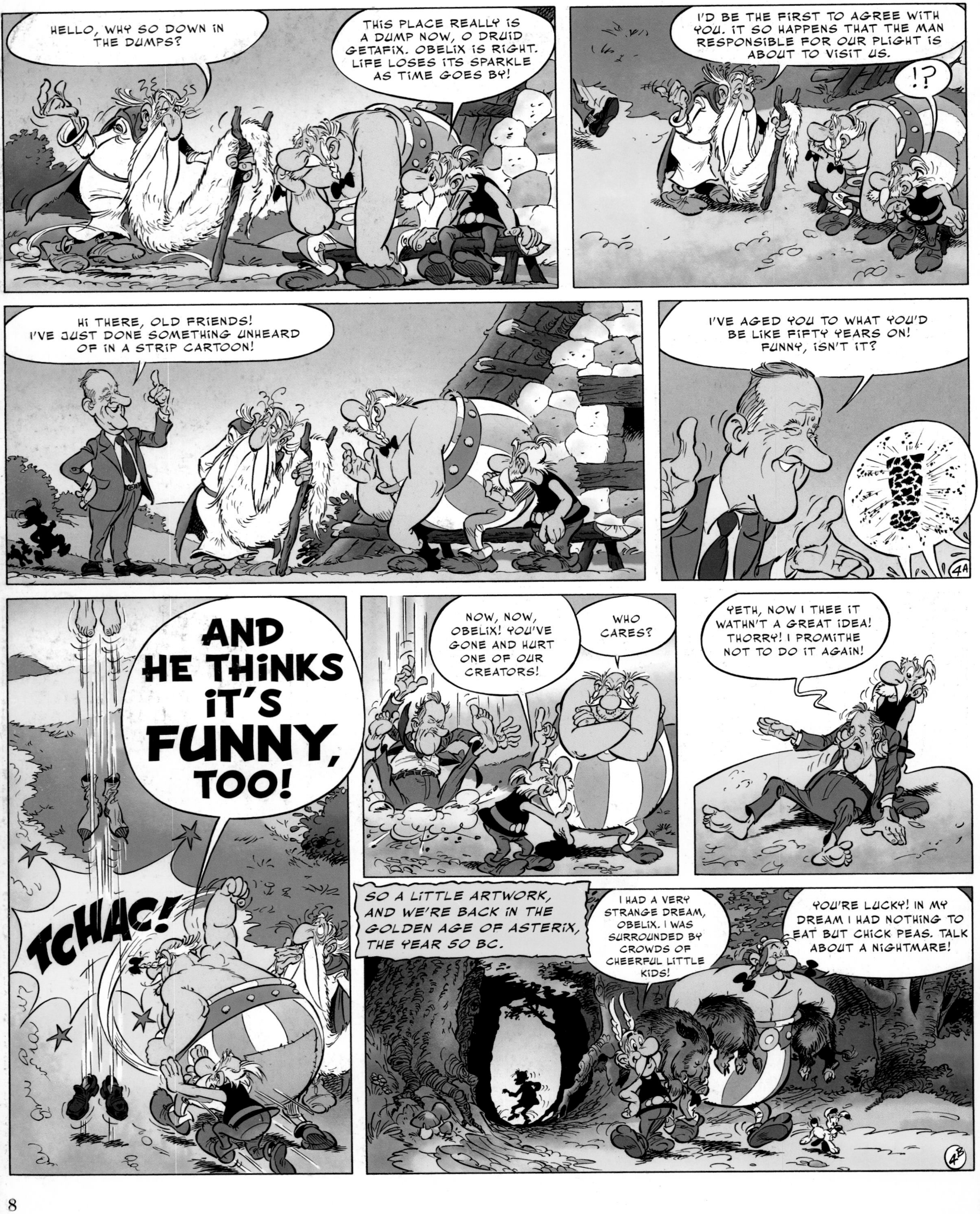
HELLO, WHY SO DOWN IN THE DUMPS?
THIS PLACE REALLY IS A DUMP NOW, O DRUID GETAFIX. OBELIX IS RIGHT. LIFE LOSES ITS SPARKLE AS TIME GOES BY!
I'D BE THE FIRST TO AGREE WITH YOU. IT SO HAPPENS THAT THE MAN RESPONSIBLE FOR OUR PLIGHT IS ABOUT TO VISIT US.
!?
HI THERE, OLD FRIENDS! I'VE JUST DONE SOMETHING UNHEARD OF IN A STRIP CARTOON!
I'VE AGED YOU TO WHAT YOU'D BE LIKE FIFTY YEARS ON! FUNNY, ISN'T IT?
4A
AND HE THINKS IT'S FUNNY, TOO!
TCHAC!
NOW, NOW, OBELIX! YOU'VE GONE AND HURT ONE OF OUR CREATORS!
WHO CARES?
YETH, NOW I THEE IT WATHN'T A GREAT IDEA! THORRY! I PROMITHE NOT TO DO IT AGAIN!
SO A LITTLE ARTWORK, AND WE'RE BACK IN THE GOLDEN AGE OF ASTERIX, THE YEAR 50 BC.
I HAD A VERY STRANGE DREAM, OBELIX. I WAS SURROUNDED BY CROWDS OF CHEERFUL LITTLE KIDS!
YOU'RE LUCKY! IN MY DREAM I HAD NOTHING TO EAT BUT CHICK PEAS. TALK ABOUT A NIGHTMARE!
4B

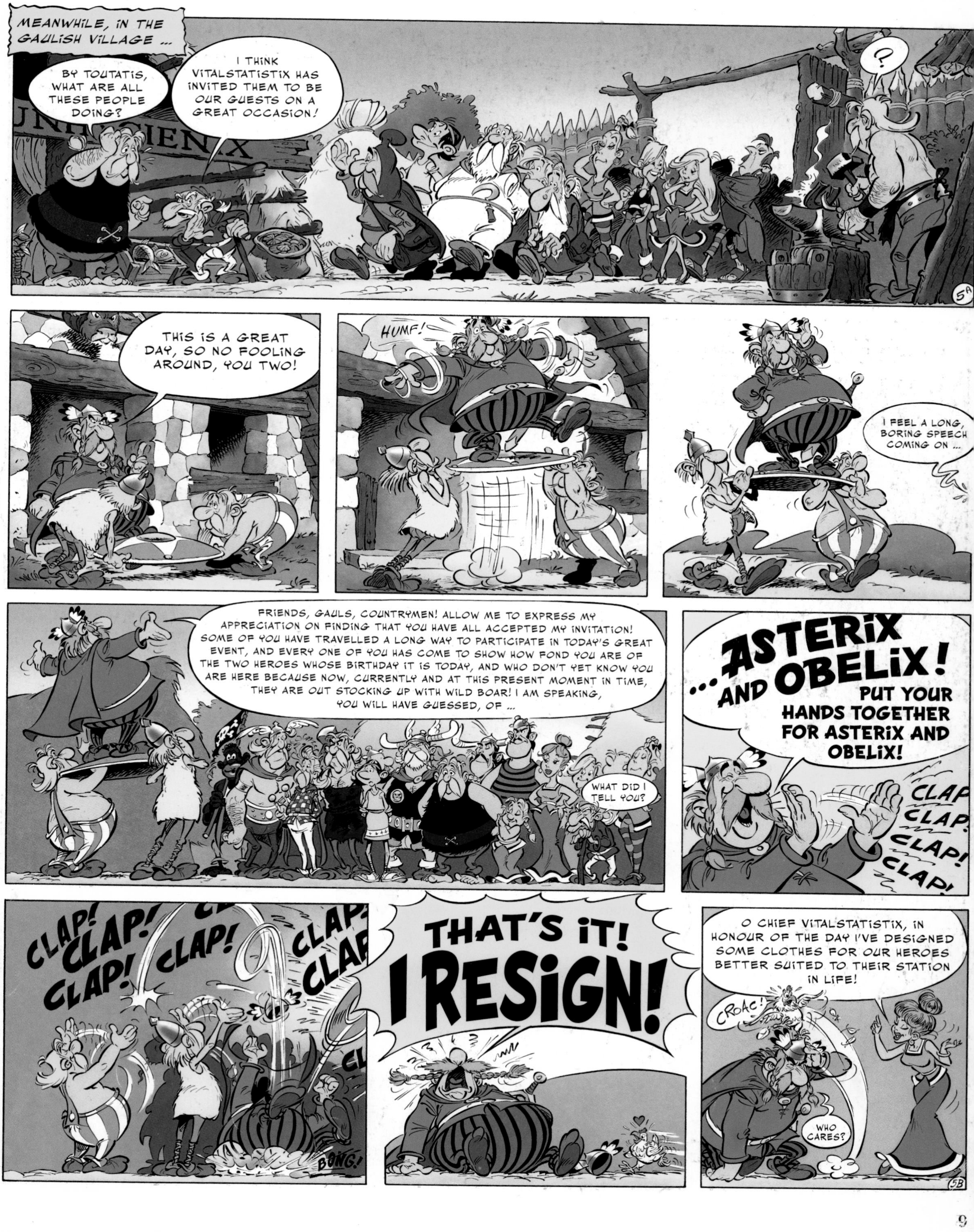
MEANWHILE, IN THE GAULISH VILLAGE ...
BY TOUTATIS, WHAT ARE ALL THESE PEOPLE DOING?
I THINK VITALSTATISTIX HAS INVITED THEM TO BE OUR GUESTS ON A GREAT OCCASION!
?
THIS IS A GREAT DAY, SO NO FOOLING AROUND, YOU TWO!
HUMF!
I FEEL A LONG, BORING SPEECH COMING ON ...
FRIENDS, GAULS, COUNTRYMEN! ALLOW ME TO EXPRESS MY APPRECIATION ON FINDING THAT YOU HAVE ALL ACCEPTED MY INVITATION! SOME OF YOU HAVE TRAVELLED A LONG WAY TO PARTICIPATE IN TODAY'S GREAT EVENT, AND EVERY ONE OF YOU HAS COME TO SHOW HOW FOND YOU ARE OF THE TWO HEROES WHOSE BIRTHDAY IT IS TODAY, AND WHO DON'T YET KNOW YOU ARE HERE BECAUSE NOW, CURRENTLY AND AT THIS PRESENT MOMENT IN TIME, THEY ARE OUT STOCKING UP WITH WILD BOAR! I AM SPEAKING, YOU WILL HAVE GUESSED, OF ...
WHAT DID I TELL YOU?
... ASTERIX AND OBELIX! PUT YOUR HANDS TOGETHER FOR ASTERIX AND OBELIX!
CLAP! CLAP! CLAP! CLAP!
CLAP! CLAP! CLAP! CLAP!
BONG!
THAT'S IT! I RESIGN!
O CHIEF VITALSTATISTIX, IN HONOUR OF THE DAY I'VE DESIGNED SOME CLOTHES FOR OUR HEROES BETTER SUITED TO THEIR STATION IN LIFE!
CROAC!
WHO CARES?

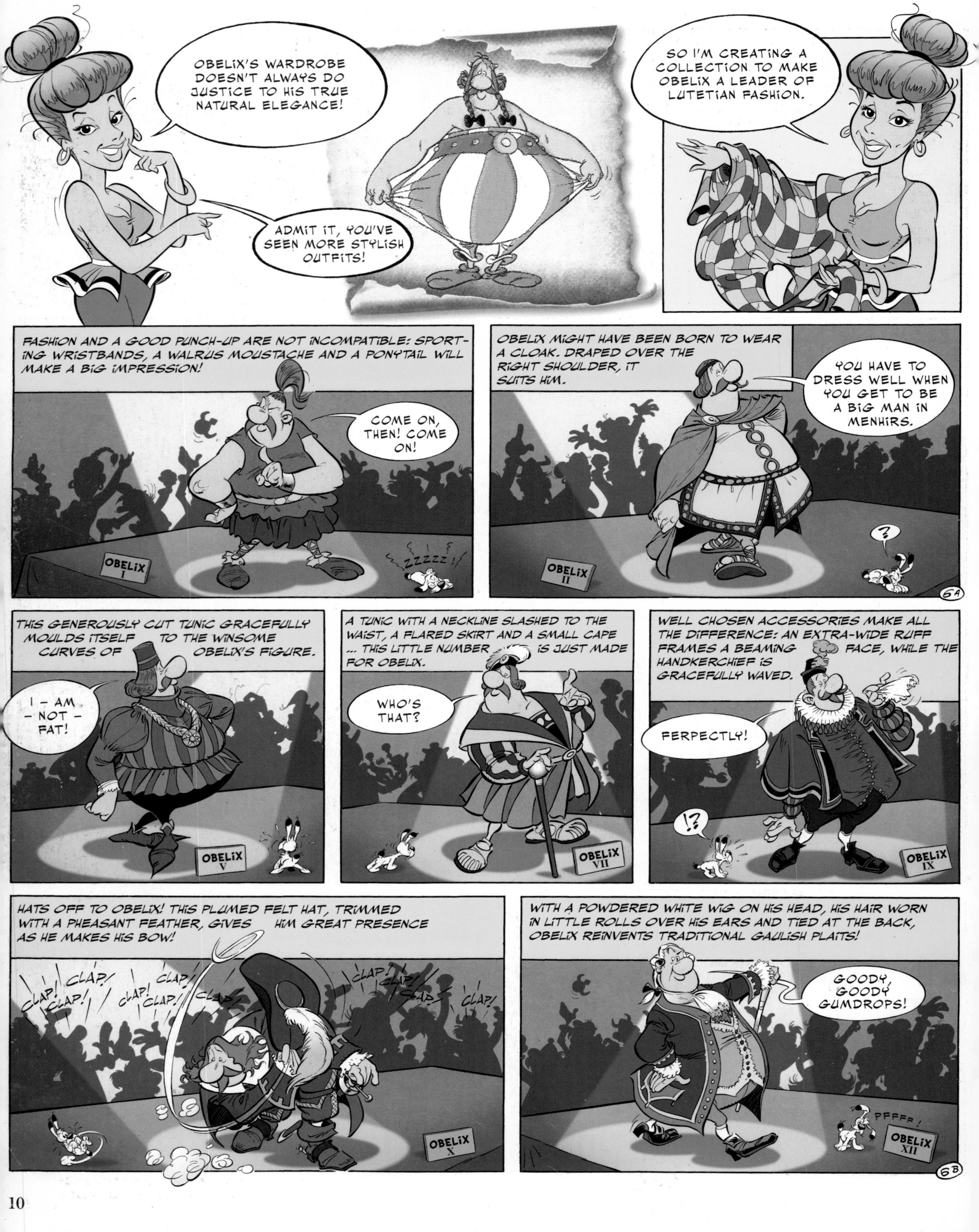

OBELIX'S WARDROBE DOESN'T ALWAYS DO JUSTICE TO HIS TRUE NATURAL ELEGANCE!
ADMIT IT, YOU'VE SEEN MORE STYLISH OUTFITS!
SO I'M CREATING A COLLECTION TO MAKE OBELIX A LEADER OF LUTETIAN FASHION.
FASHION AND A GOOD PUNCH-UP ARE NOT INCOMPATIBLE: SPORTING WRISTBANDS, A WALRUS MOUSTACHE AND A PONYTAIL WILL MAKE A BIG IMPRESSION!
COME ON, THEN! COME ON!
ZZZZZ!
OBELIX I
OBELIX MIGHT HAVE BEEN BORN TO WEAR A CLOAK. DRAPED OVER THE RIGHT SHOULDER, IT SUITS HIM.
YOU HAVE TO DRESS WELL WHEN YOU GET TO BE A BIG MAN IN MENHIRS.
?
OBELIX II
6A
THIS GENEROUSLY CUT TUNIC GRACEFULLY MOULDS ITSELF TO THE WINSOME CURVES OF OBELIX'S FIGURE.
I – AM – NOT – FAT!
OBELIX V
A TUNIC WITH A NECKLINE SLASHED TO THE WAIST, A FLARED SKIRT AND A SMALL CAPE ... THIS LITTLE NUMBER IS JUST MADE FOR OBELIX.
WHO'S THAT?
OBELIX VII
WELL CHOSEN ACCESSORIES MAKE ALL THE DIFFERENCE: AN EXTRA-WIDE RUFF FRAMES A BEAMING FACE, WHILE THE HANDKERCHIEF IS GRACEFULLY WAVED.
FERPECTLY!
!?
OBELIX IX
HATS OFF TO OBELIX! THIS PLUMED FELT HAT, TRIMMED WITH A PHEASANT FEATHER, GIVES HIM GREAT PRESENCE AS HE MAKES HIS BOW!
CLAP! CLAP! CLAP! CLAP! CLAP! CLAP! CLAP! CLAP! CLAP! CLAP! CLAP!
OBELIX X
WITH A POWDERED WHITE WIG ON HIS HEAD, HIS HAIR WORN IN LITTLE ROLLS OVER HIS EARS AND TIED AT THE BACK, OBELIX REINVENTS TRADITIONAL GAULISH PLAITS!
GOODY, GOODY GUMDROPS!
PFFFFF!
OBELIX XII
6B

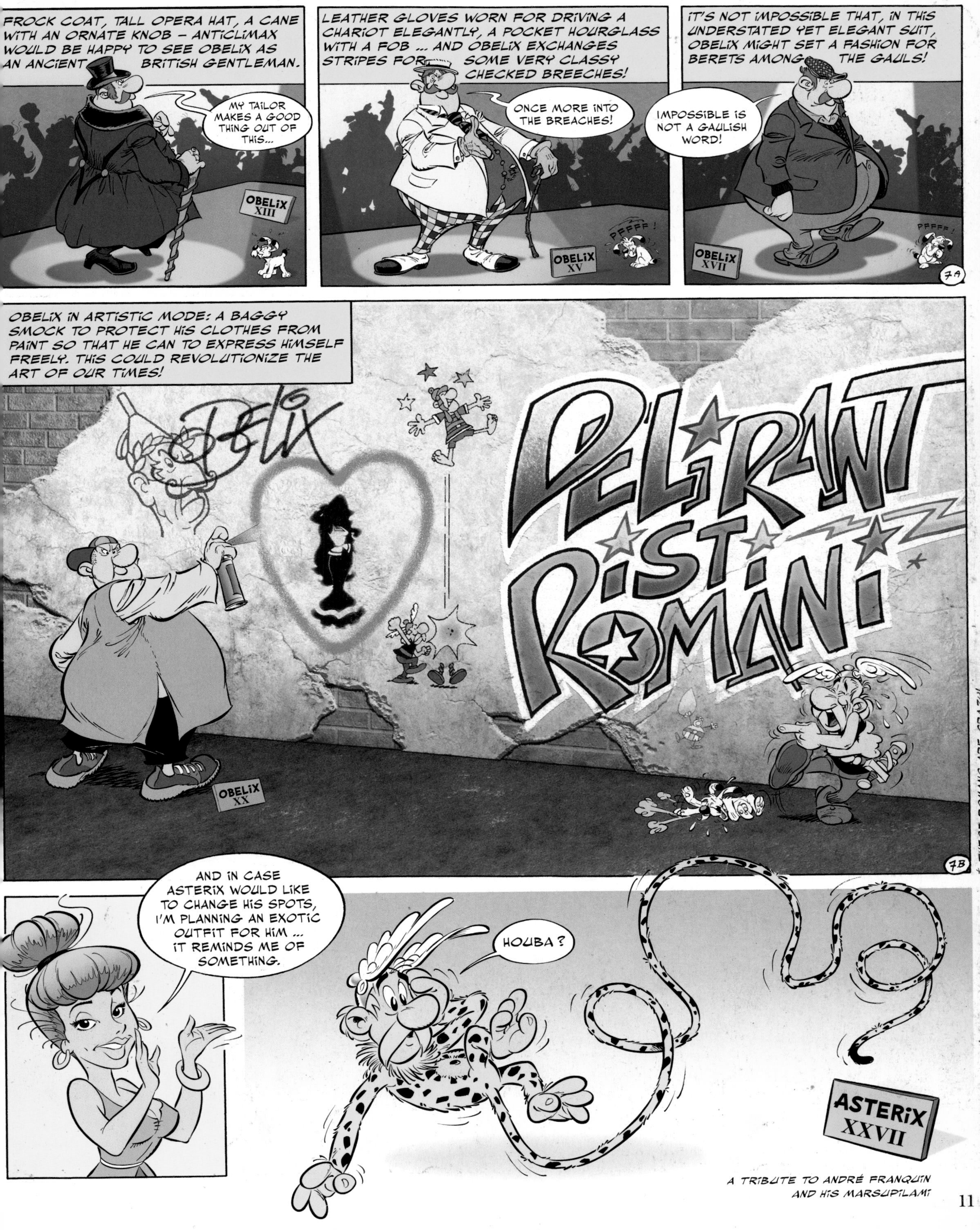
FROCK COAT, TALL OPERA HAT, A CANE WITH AN ORNATE KNOB – ANTICLIMAX WOULD BE HAPPY TO SEE OBELIX AS AN ANCIENT BRITISH GENTLEMAN.
MY TAILOR MAKES A GOOD THING OUT OF THIS...
OBELIX XIII
LEATHER GLOVES WORN FOR DRIVING A CHARIOT ELEGANTLY, A POCKET HOURGLASS WITH A FOB ... AND OBELIX EXCHANGES STRIPES FOR SOME VERY CLASSY CHECKED BREECHES!
ONCE MORE INTO THE BREACHES!
PFFFFF!
OBELIX XV
IT'S NOT IMPOSSIBLE THAT, IN THIS UNDERSTATED YET ELEGANT SUIT, OBELIX MIGHT SET A FASHION FOR BERETS AMONG THE GAULS!
IMPOSSIBLE IS NOT A GAULISH WORD!
PFFFFF!
OBELIX XVII
7A
OBELIX IN ARTISTIC MODE: A BAGGY SMOCK TO PROTECT HIS CLOTHES FROM PAINT SO THAT HE CAN TO EXPRESS HIMSELF FREELY. THIS COULD REVOLUTIONIZE THE ART OF OUR TIMES!
OBELIX
DELIRANT iST ROMANi
OBELIX XX
7B
AND IN CASE ASTERIX WOULD LIKE TO CHANGE HIS SPOTS, I'M PLANNING AN EXOTIC OUTFIT FOR HIM ... IT REMINDS ME OF SOMETHING.
HOUBA ?
ASTERIX XXVII

A TRIBUTE TO ANDRÉ FRANQUIN AND HIS MARSUPILAMI

* THESE ROMANS ARE CRAZY!

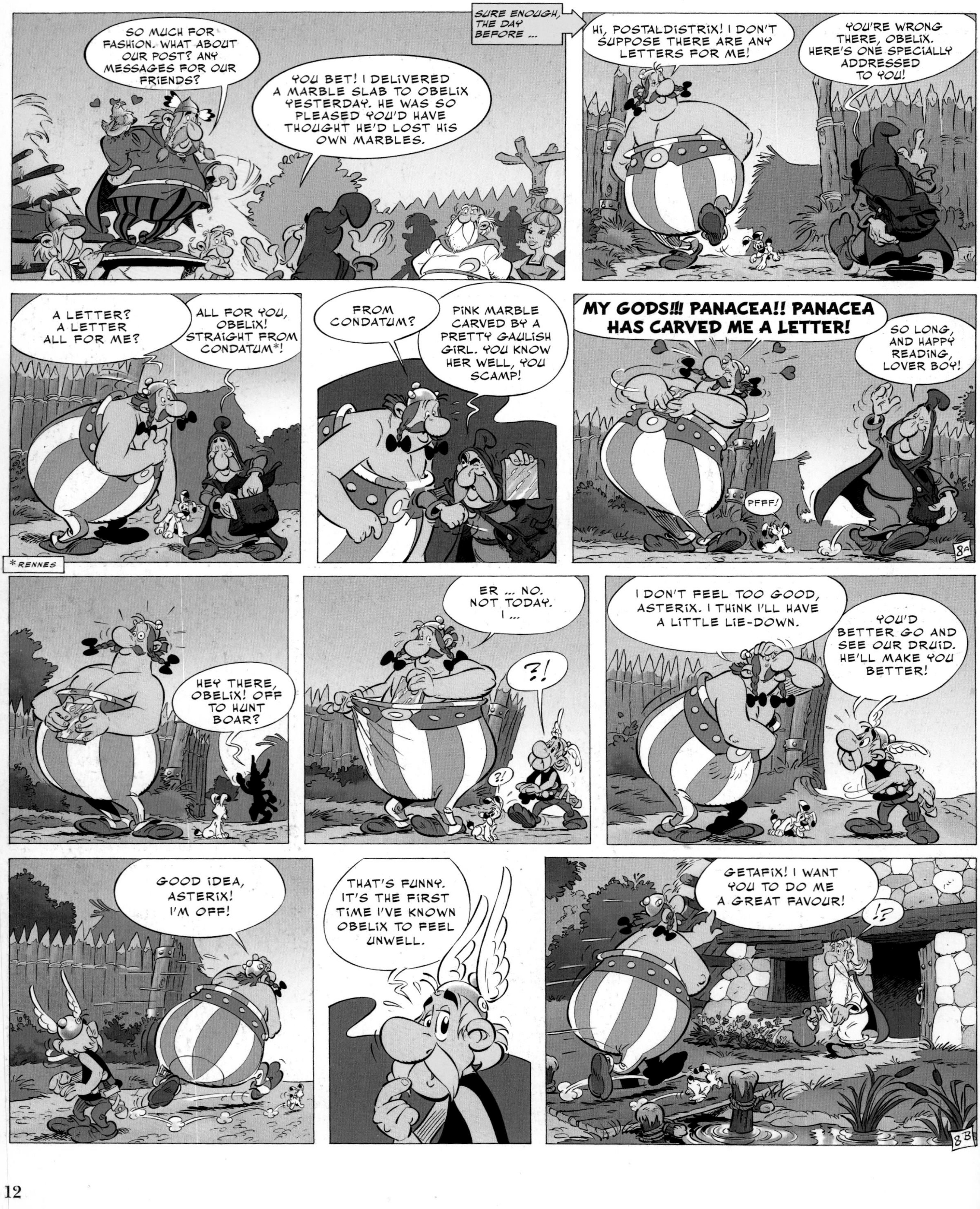
SO MUCH FOR FASHION. WHAT ABOUT OUR POST? ANY MESSAGES FOR OUR FRIENDS?
YOU BET! I DELIVERED A MARBLE SLAB TO OBELIX YESTERDAY. HE WAS SO PLEASED YOU'D HAVE THOUGHT HE'D LOST HIS OWN MARBLES.
SURE ENOUGH, THE DAY BEFORE ...
HI, POSTALDISTRIX! I DON'T SUPPOSE THERE ARE ANY LETTERS FOR ME!
YOU'RE WRONG THERE, OBELIX. HERE'S ONE SPECIALLY ADDRESSED TO YOU!
A LETTER? A LETTER ALL FOR ME?
ALL FOR YOU, OBELIX! STRAIGHT FROM CONDATUM*!
FROM CONDATUM?
PINK MARBLE CARVED BY A PRETTY GAULISH GIRL. YOU KNOW HER WELL, YOU SCAMP!
MY GODS!!! PANACEA!! PANACEA HAS CARVED ME A LETTER!
SO LONG, AND HAPPY READING, LOVER BOY!
PFFF!
8A
*RENNES
HEY THERE, OBELIX! OFF TO HUNT BOAR?
ER ... NO. NOT TODAY. I ...
?!
?!
I DON'T FEEL TOO GOOD, ASTERIX. I THINK I'LL HAVE A LITTLE LIE-DOWN.
YOU'D BETTER GO AND SEE OUR DRUID. HE'LL MAKE YOU BETTER!
GOOD IDEA, ASTERIX! I'M OFF!
THAT'S FUNNY. IT'S THE FIRST TIME I'VE KNOWN OBELIX TO FEEL UNWELL.
GETAFIX! I WANT YOU TO DO ME A GREAT FAVOUR!
!?
8B

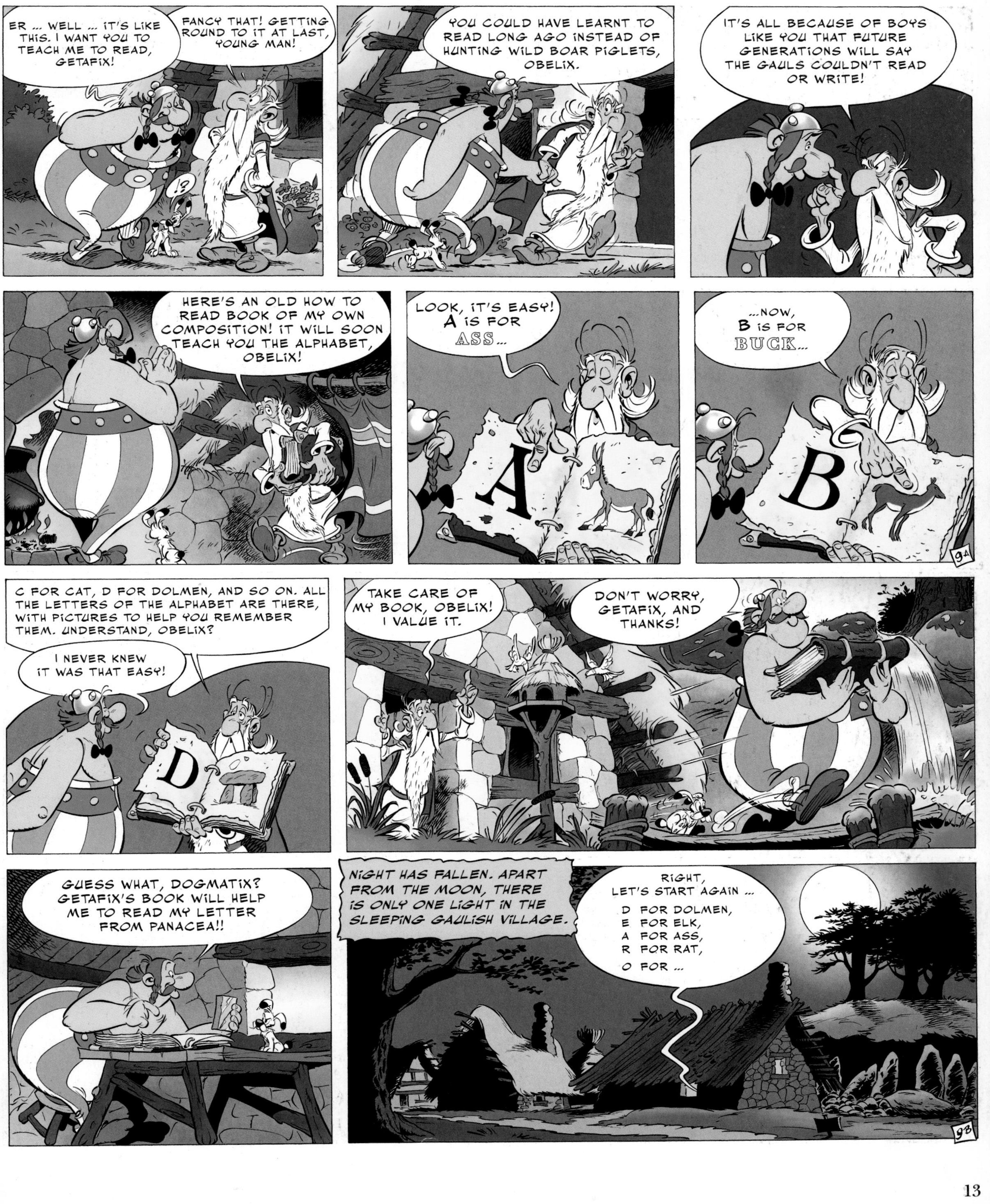

ER ... WELL ... IT'S LIKE THIS. I WANT YOU TO TEACH ME TO READ, GETAFIX!
FANCY THAT! GETTING ROUND TO IT AT LAST, YOUNG MAN!
YOU COULD HAVE LEARNT TO READ LONG AGO INSTEAD OF HUNTING WILD BOAR PIGLETS, OBELIX.
IT'S ALL BECAUSE OF BOYS LIKE YOU THAT FUTURE GENERATIONS WILL SAY THE GAULS COULDN'T READ OR WRITE!
HERE'S AN OLD HOW TO READ BOOK OF MY OWN COMPOSITION! IT WILL SOON TEACH YOU THE ALPHABET, OBELIX!
LOOK, IT'S EASY! A IS FOR ASS...
A
...NOW, B IS FOR BUCK...
B
C FOR CAT, D FOR DOLMEN, AND SO ON. ALL THE LETTERS OF THE ALPHABET ARE THERE, WITH PICTURES TO HELP YOU REMEMBER THEM. UNDERSTAND, OBELIX?
I NEVER KNEW IT WAS THAT EASY!
D
TAKE CARE OF MY BOOK, OBELIX! I VALUE IT.
DON'T WORRY, GETAFIX, AND THANKS!
GUESS WHAT, DOGMATIX? GETAFIX'S BOOK WILL HELP ME TO READ MY LETTER FROM PANACEA!!
NIGHT HAS FALLEN. APART FROM THE MOON, THERE IS ONLY ONE LIGHT IN THE SLEEPING GAULISH VILLAGE.
RIGHT, LET'S START AGAIN ... D FOR DOLMEN, E FOR ELK, A FOR ASS, R FOR RAT, O FOR ...

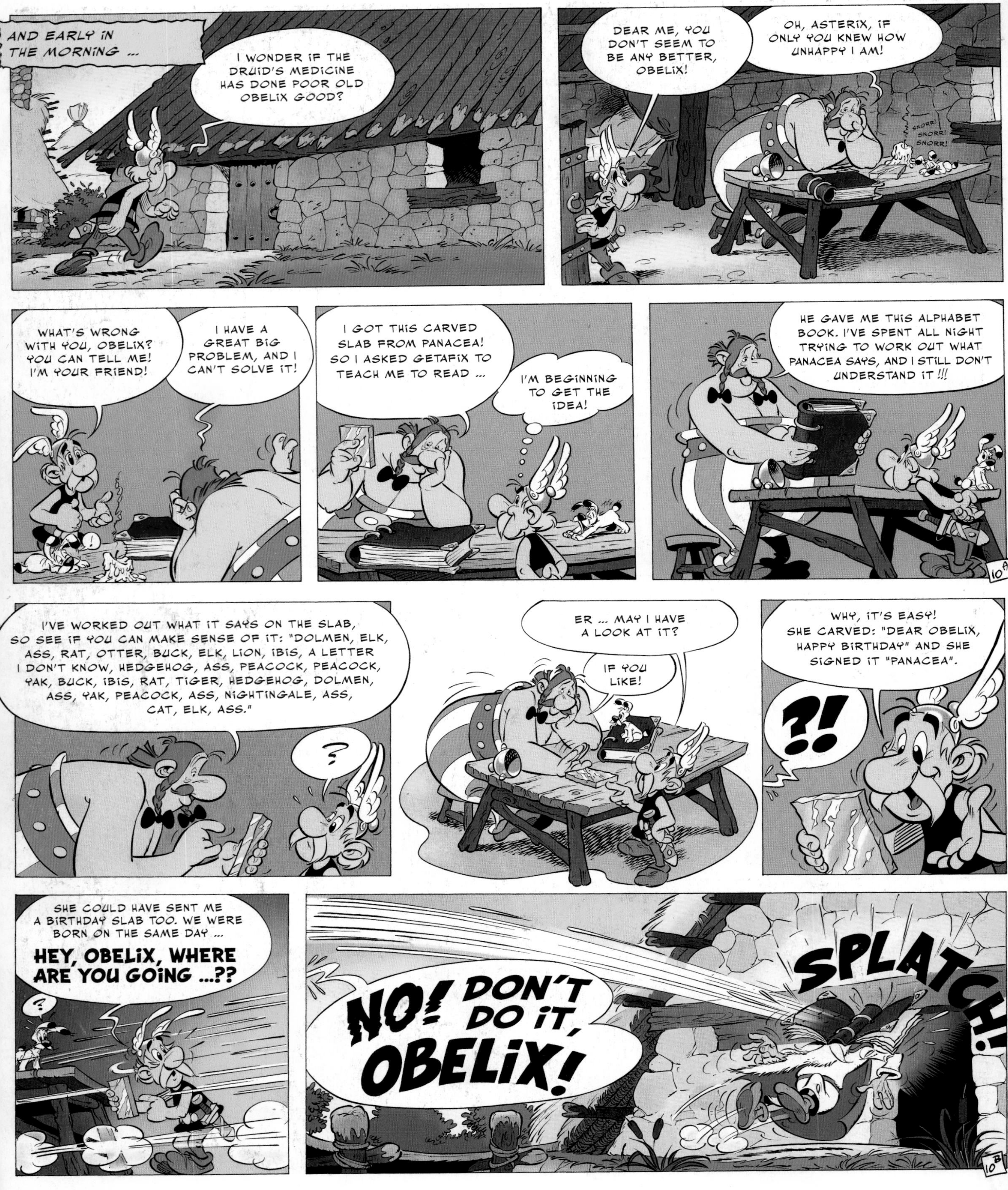
AND EARLY IN THE MORNING ...
I WONDER IF THE DRUID'S MEDICINE HAS DONE POOR OLD OBELIX GOOD?
DEAR ME, YOU DON'T SEEM TO BE ANY BETTER, OBELIX!
OH, ASTERIX, IF ONLY YOU KNEW HOW UNHAPPY I AM!
SNORR! SNORR! SNORR!
WHAT'S WRONG WITH YOU, OBELIX? YOU CAN TELL ME! I'M YOUR FRIEND!
I HAVE A GREAT BIG PROBLEM, AND I CAN'T SOLVE IT!
I GOT THIS CARVED SLAB FROM PANACEA! SO I ASKED GETAFIX TO TEACH ME TO READ ...
I'M BEGINNING TO GET THE IDEA!
HE GAVE ME THIS ALPHABET BOOK. I'VE SPENT ALL NIGHT TRYING TO WORK OUT WHAT PANACEA SAYS, AND I STILL DON'T UNDERSTAND IT !!!
10A
I'VE WORKED OUT WHAT IT SAYS ON THE SLAB, SO SEE IF YOU CAN MAKE SENSE OF IT: "DOLMEN, ELK, ASS, RAT, OTTER, BUCK, ELK, LION, IBIS, A LETTER I DON'T KNOW, HEDGEHOG, ASS, PEACOCK, PEACOCK, YAK, BUCK, IBIS, RAT, TIGER, HEDGEHOG, DOLMEN, ASS, YAK, PEACOCK, ASS, NIGHTINGALE, ASS, CAT, ELK, ASS."
?
ER ... MAY I HAVE A LOOK AT IT?
IF YOU LIKE!
WHY, IT'S EASY! SHE CARVED: "DEAR OBELIX, HAPPY BIRTHDAY" AND SHE SIGNED IT "PANACEA".
?!
SHE COULD HAVE SENT ME A BIRTHDAY SLAB TOO. WE WERE BORN ON THE SAME DAY ...
HEY, OBELIX, WHERE ARE YOU GOING ...??
?
NO! DON'T DO IT, OBELIX!
SPLATCH!
10B

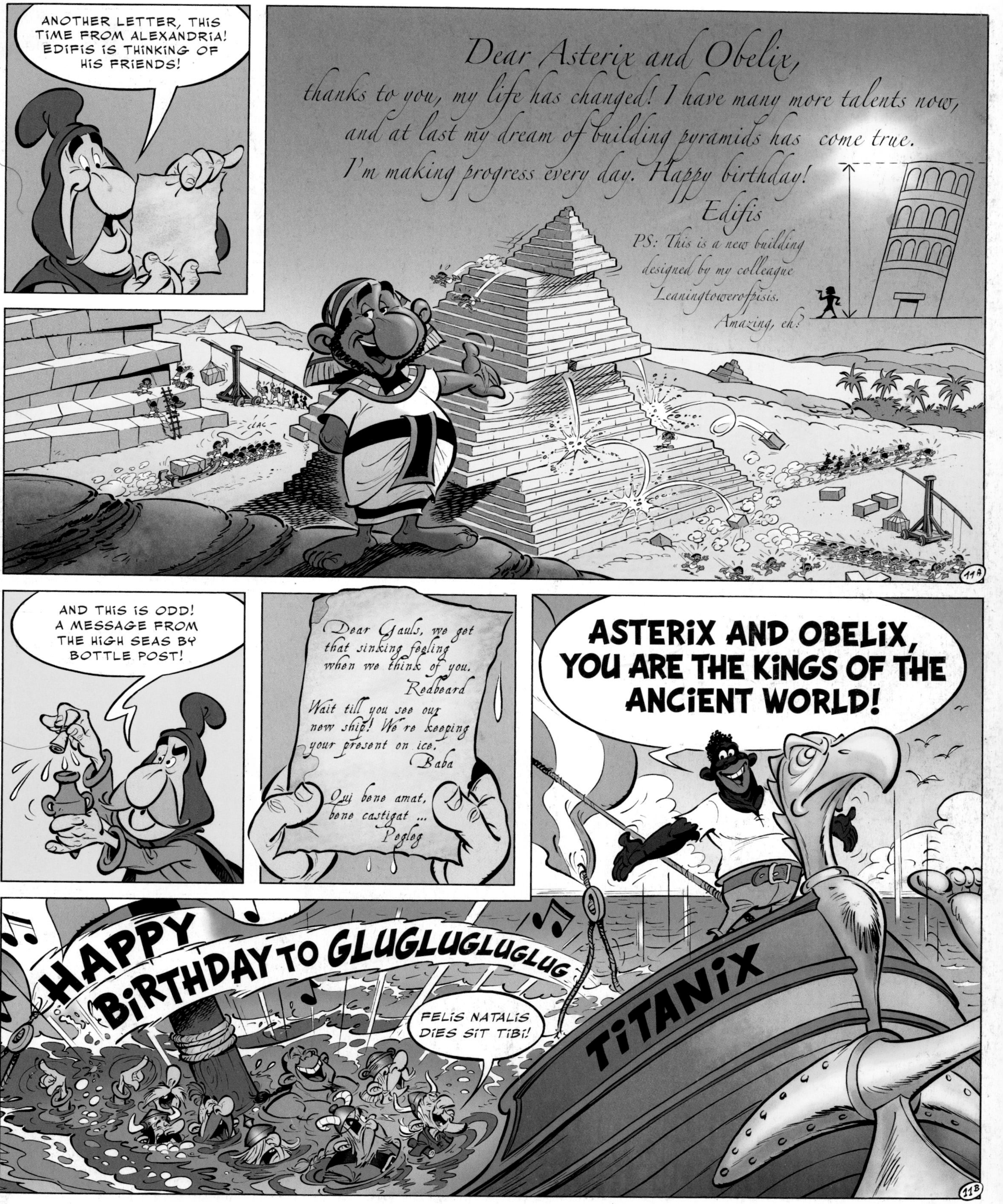
ANOTHER LETTER, THIS TIME FROM ALEXANDRIA! EDIFIS IS THINKING OF HIS FRIENDS!
Dear Asterix and Obelix,
thanks to you, my life has changed! I have many more talents now, and at last my dream of building pyramids has come true. I'm making progress every day. Happy birthday!
Edifis
PS: This is a new building designed by my colleague Leaningtowerofpisis. Amazing, eh?
AND THIS IS ODD! A MESSAGE FROM THE HIGH SEAS BY BOTTLE POST!
Dear Gauls, we get that sinking feeling when we think of you.
Redbeard
Wait till you see our new ship! We're keeping your present on ice.
Baba
Qui bene amat, bene castigat ...
Pegleg
ASTERIX AND OBELIX, YOU ARE THE KINGS OF THE ANCIENT WORLD!
HAPPY BIRTHDAY TO GLUGLUGLUGLUG
FELIS NATALIS DIES SIT TIBI!
TITANIX

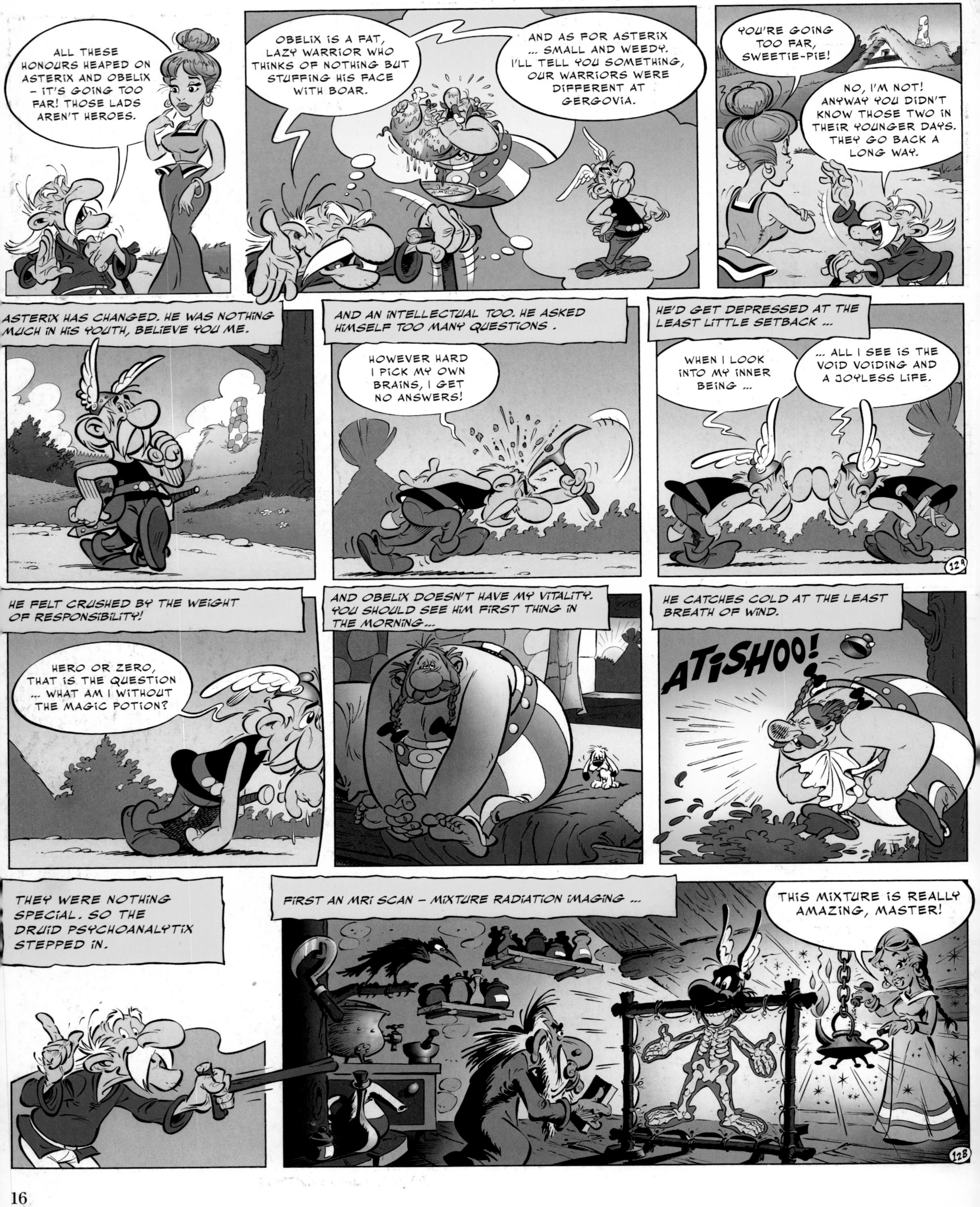

ALL THESE HONOURS HEAPED ON ASTERIX AND OBELIX – IT'S GOING TOO FAR! THOSE LADS AREN'T HEROES.
OBELIX IS A FAT, LAZY WARRIOR WHO THINKS OF NOTHING BUT STUFFING HIS FACE WITH BOAR.
AND AS FOR ASTERIX ... SMALL AND WEEDY. I'LL TELL YOU SOMETHING, OUR WARRIORS WERE DIFFERENT AT GERGOVIA.
YOU'RE GOING TOO FAR, SWEETIE-PIE!
NO, I'M NOT! ANYWAY YOU DIDN'T KNOW THOSE TWO IN THEIR YOUNGER DAYS. THEY GO BACK A LONG WAY.
ASTERIX HAS CHANGED. HE WAS NOTHING MUCH IN HIS YOUTH, BELIEVE YOU ME.
AND AN INTELLECTUAL TOO. HE ASKED HIMSELF TOO MANY QUESTIONS .
HOWEVER HARD I PICK MY OWN BRAINS, I GET NO ANSWERS!
HE'D GET DEPRESSED AT THE LEAST LITTLE SETBACK ...
WHEN I LOOK INTO MY INNER BEING ...
... ALL I SEE IS THE VOID VOIDING AND A JOYLESS LIFE.
12A
HE FELT CRUSHED BY THE WEIGHT OF RESPONSIBILITY!
HERO OR ZERO, THAT IS THE QUESTION ... WHAT AM I WITHOUT THE MAGIC POTION?
AND OBELIX DOESN'T HAVE MY VITALITY. YOU SHOULD SEE HIM FIRST THING IN THE MORNING...
HE CATCHES COLD AT THE LEAST BREATH OF WIND.
ATISHOO!
THEY WERE NOTHING SPECIAL. SO THE DRUID PSYCHOANALYTIX STEPPED IN.
FIRST AN MRI SCAN – MIXTURE RADIATION IMAGING ...
THIS MIXTURE IS REALLY AMAZING, MASTER!
12B

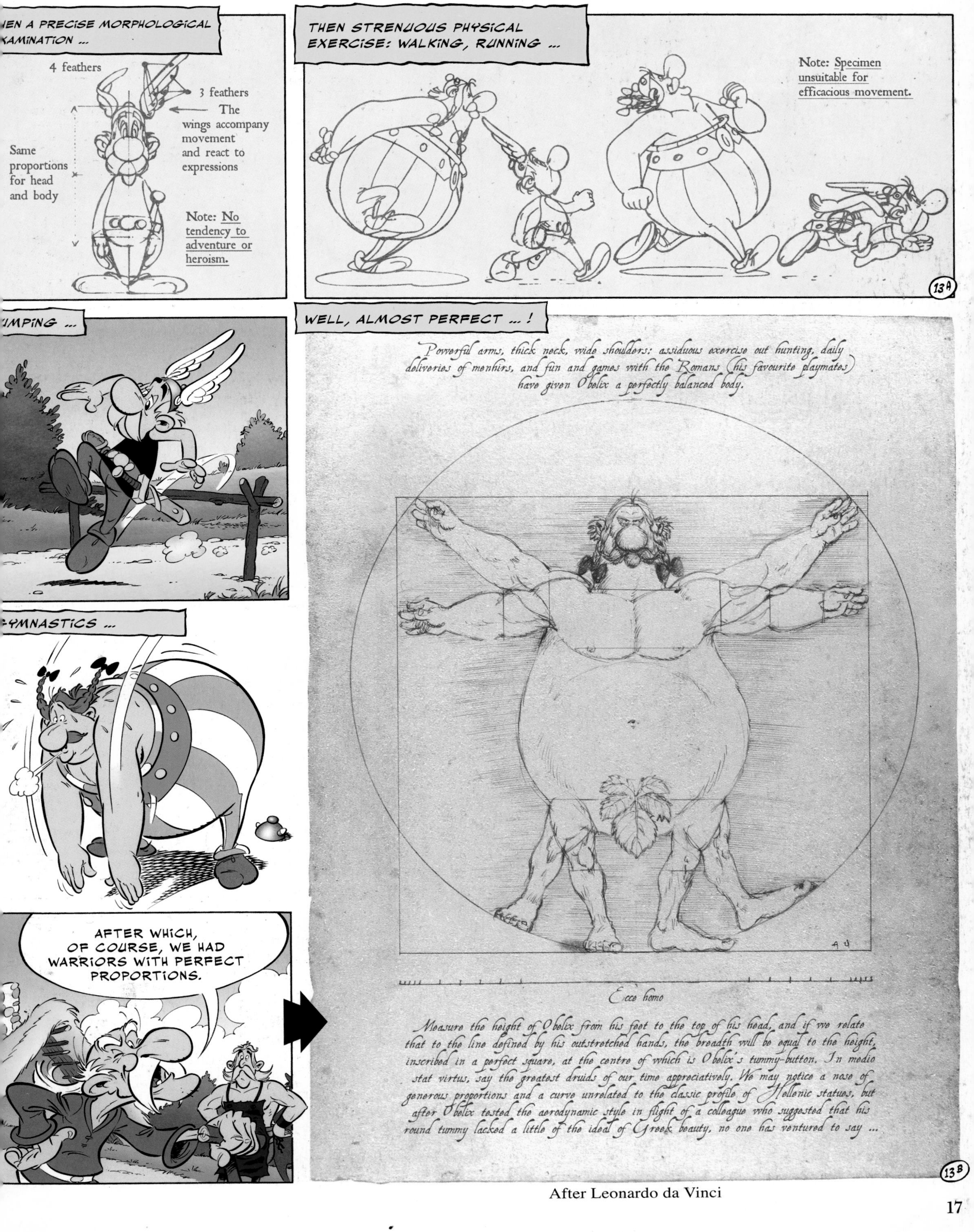
EN A PRECISE MORPHOLOGICAL
AMINATION ...
4 feathers
3 feathers
The wings accompany movement and react to expressions
Same proportions for head and body
Note: No tendency to adventure or heroism.
THEN STRENUOUS PHYSICAL EXERCISE: WALKING, RUNNING ...
Note: Specimen unsuitable for efficacious movement.
13A
MPING ...
WELL, ALMOST PERFECT ... !
Powerful arms, thick neck, wide shoulders: assiduous exercise out hunting, daily deliveries of menhirs, and fun and games with the Romans (his favourite playmates) have given Obelix a perfectly balanced body.
Ecce homo
Measure the height of Obelix from his feet to the top of his head, and if we relate that to the line defined by his outstretched hands, the breadth will be equal to the height, inscribed in a perfect square, at the centre of which is Obelix's tummy-button. In medio stat virtus, say the greatest druids of our time appreciatively. We may notice a nose of generous proportions and a curve unrelated to the classic profile of Hellenic statues, but after Obelix tested the aerodynamic style in flight of a colleague who suggested that his round tummy lacked a little of the ideal of Greek beauty, no one has ventured to say ...
YMNASTICS ...
AFTER WHICH, OF COURSE, WE HAD WARRIORS WITH PERFECT PROPORTIONS.
13B
After Leonardo da Vinci

OH, COME OFF IT, GERIATRIX ... ASTERIX AND OBELIX AREN'T DECREPIT YET!
THAT'S TRUE. THEY KEEP TRAVELLING, AND TRAVEL FORMS YOUNG MINDS, RIGHT?
EXACTLY! AND I KNOW ALL ABOUT FOREIGN TRAVEL!
I'M GIVING OUR FRIENDS THIS TRAVEL GUIDE. THEY'LL LIKE IT!
?

YEAR L BC EDITION

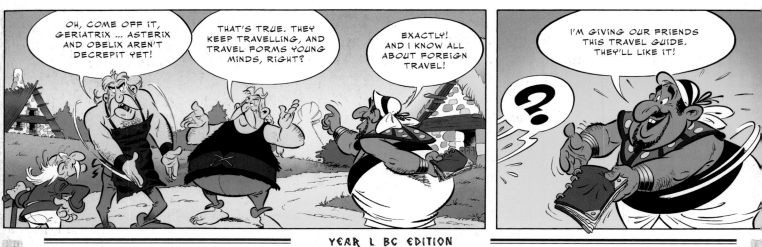

# THE CIRCUMBENDIBUS TRAVEL GUIDE[1]

## Gauls, do you like to travel? If so our guide, written by an Armorican adventurer, is just the book for you!

Of course the Gauls like to travel, by Toutatis! Here in the village, of course, we don't have far to go. The beach is very close, and there's the forest just inland. All the pleasures of a good holiday can be found here: the seaside with its pirates, mushroom-picking, boar-hunting, and a good laugh with Roman patrols. Not to mention that here in Armorica we have a very invigorating climate. In short, it's rather like being on holiday all the year round for the Romans and us.

### THE PLEASURES OF THE SEASIDE PIRATES

BOARDING PIRATE VESSELS IS NOT INCLUDED IN THE FARE. IT'S AN EXTRA.
?
?
WHAT D'YOU MEAN, AN EXTRA?
I'D JUST LIKE TO POINT OUT THAT BOARDING IS AN OPTIONAL EXTRA ...
APPLY TO THE PURSER. IT'S TWO SESTERTII.

Frames from *Asterix at the Olympic Games*

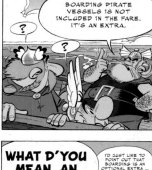

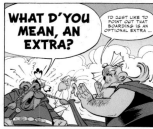

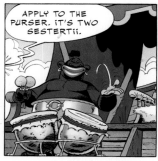

*To avoid inconvenience, follow the advice in the* ***Cicumbendibus Guide*** *when booking your holiday.*

### LEISURE ACTIVITIES ON HOLIDAY

A RELAXING MOMENT ON AN ARMORICAN BEACH

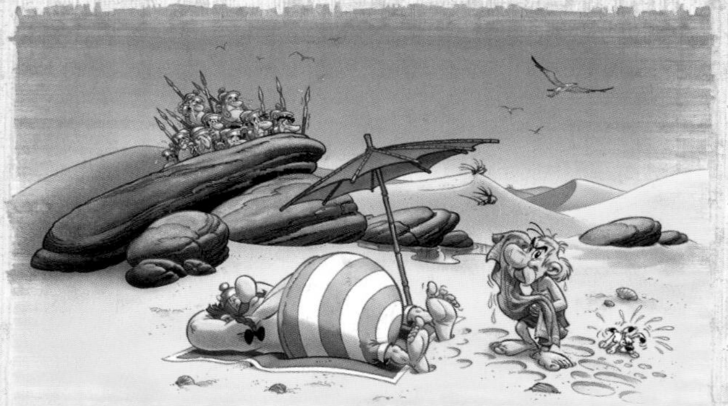

*A bracing climate, lovely blue skies ... and lifeguards on the watch!*

### FUN AND GAMES WITH FRIENDS

OBELIX !?
WE DO LIKE TO BE BESIDE THE SEASIDE, OH, WE DO LIKE TO BE BESIDE THE SEA ...
THESE ROMANS MAY BE CRAZY, BUT I WOULDN'T LIKE TO GO AWAY WITHOUT THEM.

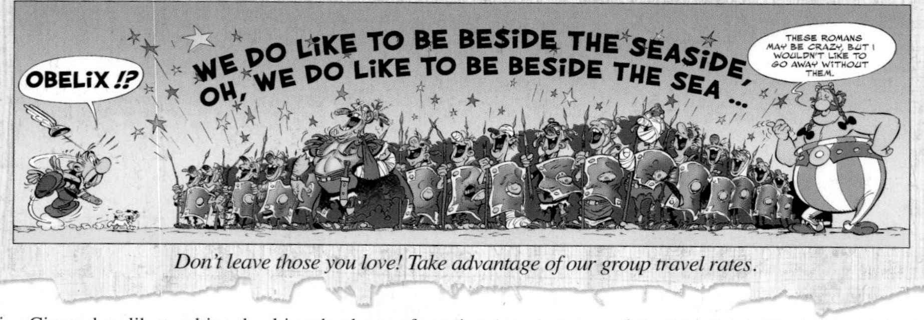

*Don't leave those you love! Take advantage of our group travel rates.*

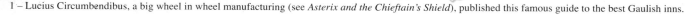

1 – Lucius Circumbendibus, a big wheel in wheel manufacturing (see *Asterix and the Chieftain's Shield*), published this famous guide to the best Gaulish inns.

Those of our countrymen who aren't so lucky, meaning everyone else, start thinking about their holidays in the month of Januarius[1] onwards. If you want to go away in Quintilis[2] or Sextilis[3] you have to plan in advance. After the month of Aprilis[4] there are no seaside villas left to be booked along the coast, and the only subject of conversation is what the weather will be like in summer. ("Mind you, there's a lot of climate change these days. All those Roman war machines will make the sky fall on our heads one of these days!")

Some people disapprove of this attitude. "What's Gaul coming to?" they ask. "In the good old days people thought of work and nothing but work!" But even these sensible souls are not the last to set out for the southern provinces. It's the beaches of the Middle Sea that attract most tourists: Nicae, Antipolis, Forum Julii, Citharista, Olbia, Heraclea Caccabaria, Carsicis[5] and Athenopolis[6] are full of teeming crowds looking for pleasure all summer. (Particularly Athenopolis, frequented by people from the ancient world, the high society of Lutetia, and the beatnix, those strange barbarians who don't plait or wash their long hair. Some say they're like that after getting nicely stoned at Nicae.)

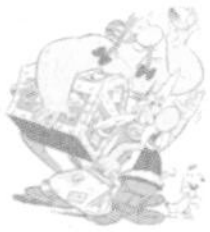

1 – January

2 – Soon to be called Julius in honour of Caesar, and later July

3 – To be renamed Augustus and then August

4 – April

5 – Respectively: Nice, Antibes, Fréjus, La Ciotat, Hyères, Cavalaire, Cassis

6 – Small Massilian place near present-day Saint-Tropez

## GETTING ORGANIZED

*How to pack. Try to take only the essentials.*

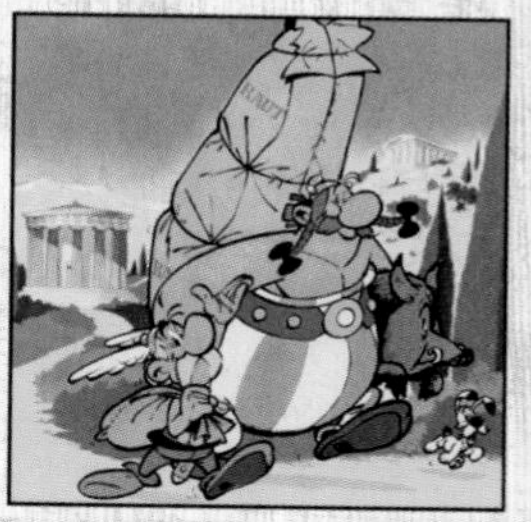

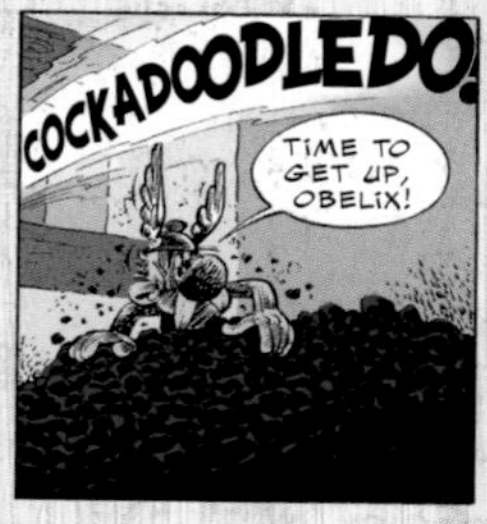
COCKADOODLEDO!
TIME TO GET UP, OBELIX!

*To avoid ending up in a shady sort of inn, reserve in advance!*

*For getting around, opt for a Gaulish-registered chariot*

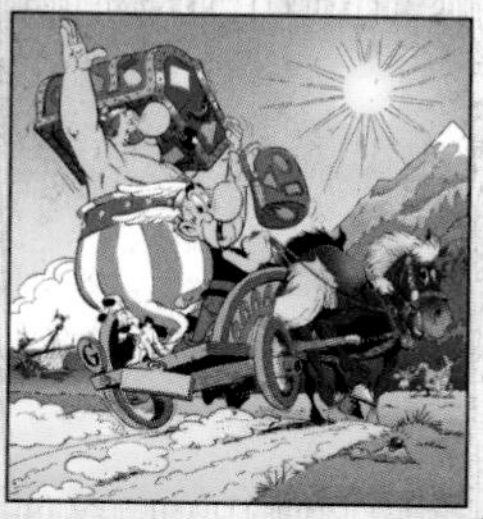

Middle frame from *Astérix and the Chieftain's Shield*

## A SUCCESSFUL DEPARTURE

*The moment comes to part and say goodbye. Sensitive souls look away!*

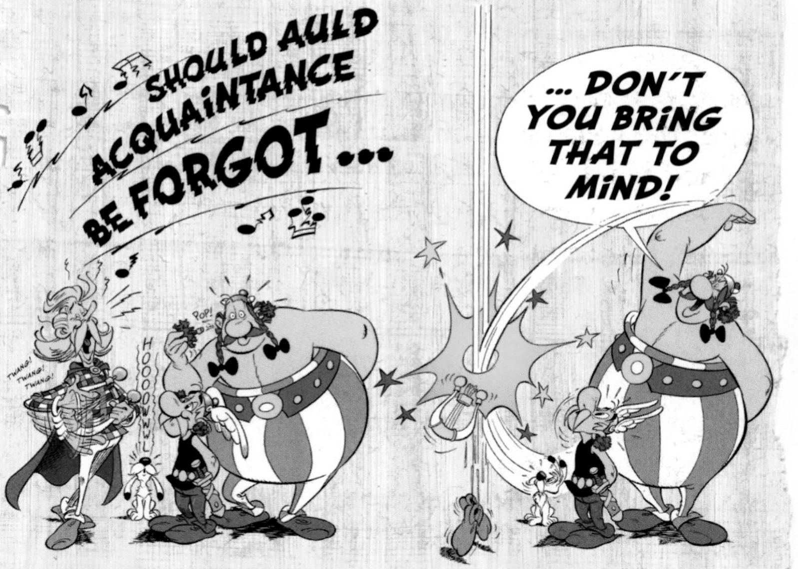
SHOULD AULD ACQUAINTANCE BE FORGOT...
... DON'T YOU BRING THAT TO MIND!
TWANG! TWANG! TWANG!
HOOOOOWWWL
POP!

## THE PLEASURES OF THE MIDDLE SEA

*A little relaxation on the beach at Nicae ...nothing like it for making new friends!*

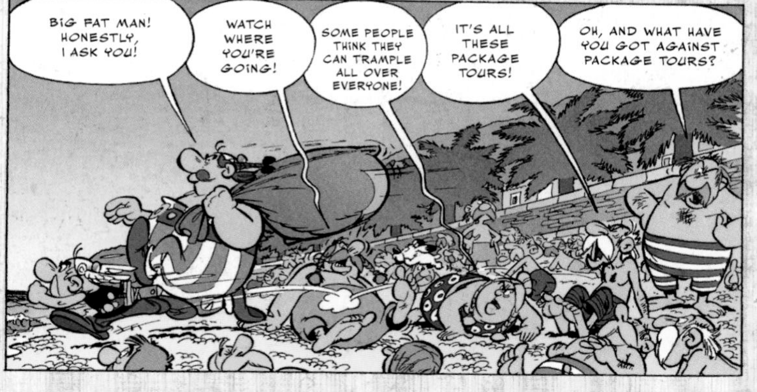
BIG FAT MAN! HONESTLY, I ASK YOU!
WATCH WHERE YOU'RE GOING!
SOME PEOPLE THINK THEY CAN TRAMPLE ALL OVER EVERYONE!
IT'S ALL THESE PACKAGE TOURS!
OH, AND WHAT HAVE YOU GOT AGAINST PACKAGE TOURS?

Frame from *Astérix and the Banquet*

Of course, the trouble is that, with everyone leaving at the same time and going the same way, the roads are crowded and, sadly, there are many accidents. Some of those are due to careless drivers hell-bent on high speed, never mind the risk to life and limb. You hear idiots saying: “Yes, old boy, Lutetia to Nicae in only three weeks non-stop!” As if two weeks more or less meant anything in a man’s life!

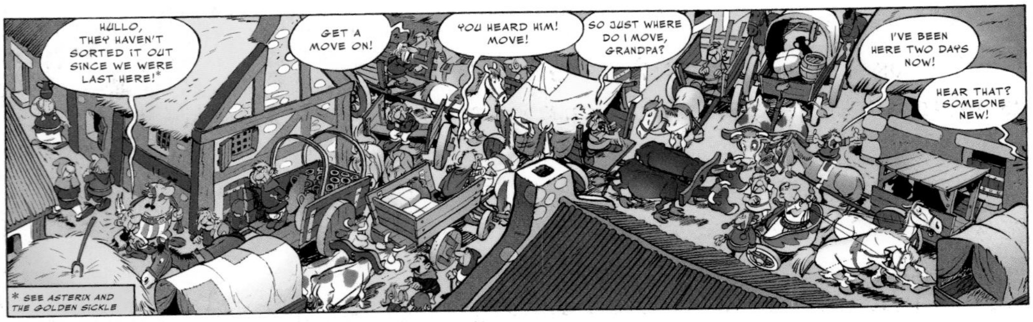
HULLO, THEY HAVEN'T SORTED IT OUT SINCE WE WERE LAST HERE!*
GET A MOVE ON!
YOU HEARD HIM! MOVE!
SO JUST WHERE DO I MOVE, GRANDPA?
I'VE BEEN HERE TWO DAYS NOW!
HEAR THAT? SOMEONE NEW!
* SEE ASTERIX AND THE GOLDEN SICKLE

Frame from *Astérix and the Banquet*

Roman patrols do their best to enforce the Pax Romana on the roads. The laws are being tightened up, and there’s talk of throwing those careless drivers who are the worst offenders to the lions, but so far that has come to nothing, and the RPOF (Roman Policing Operations Forum) is trying to impose some semblance of discipline as best it can.

# HOW TO AVOID CROWDED ROADS

**IT'S NOT IMPOSSIBLE TO AVOID CROWDED ROADS FULL OF HOLIDAY TRAFFIC AND TAILBACKS. HERE'S OUR ADVICE FOR TRAVELLING MORE EASILY.**

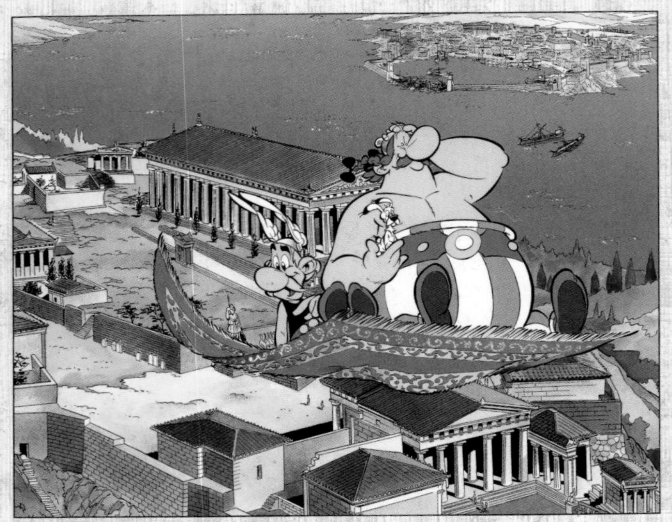

*Take to the air to avoid the holiday crowds. Travel by magic carpet!*

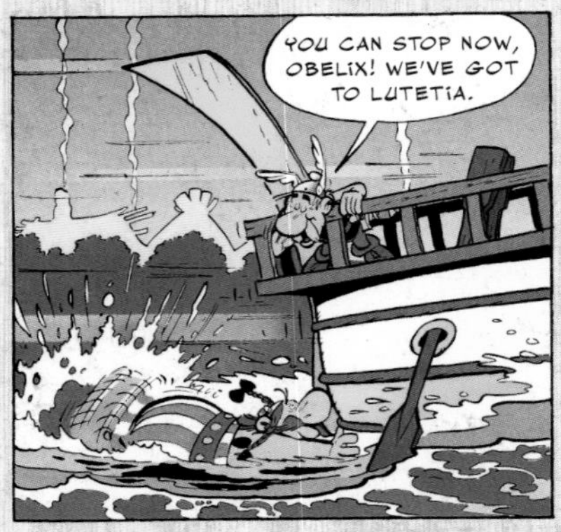
YOU CAN STOP NOW, OBELIX! WE'VE GOT TO LUTETIA.

*Travel with Obelix to avoid amphora-necks!*

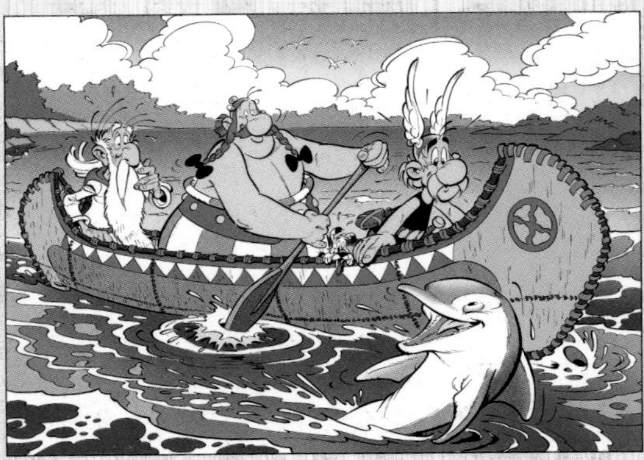

*Enjoy the peace and calm of the ocean. Travel by canoe and meet new friends.*

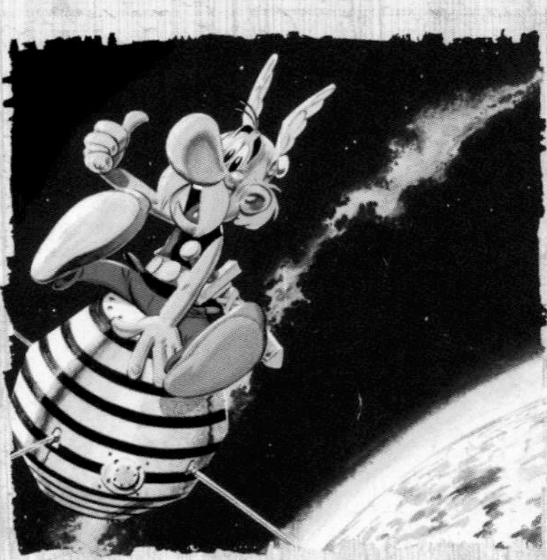

*Fly above the clouds, and cure yourself for ever of fearing that the sky will fall on your head!*

It has to be said, in defence of road users, that the design of the Roman road network is ancient. The authorities built roads paved with stone slabs which are no longer up to the pressure of modern traffic. They are cluttered up by ox-drawn haulage carts, and overtaking them is always dangerous. Nor do I think that imposing a speed limit of III millia passuum an hour[1] on all vehicles will solve the problem. And I doubt whether sending bad drivers to the Circus is a good idea, although the lions seem to think so. The roads must be widened and ring roads built around towns and villages. Anyone who has driven through Lugdunum will know what I mean.

Meanwhile people go on taking risks and suffering from road rage as they hurl insults at each other. "I'm going to barbecue those oxen of yours!" "Get going, rapa[2]-face!" "I'm not tailgating you for ever, raeda lenta[3]! Let me by!" "I'm working! I'm a slave, I am! I'm not here for fun!" "You're a slave, eh? If I was your master I'd trade you in for a donkey. Donkeys work better, they're prettier and more intelligent!" "Want to know what the donkey says to you?" And so on.

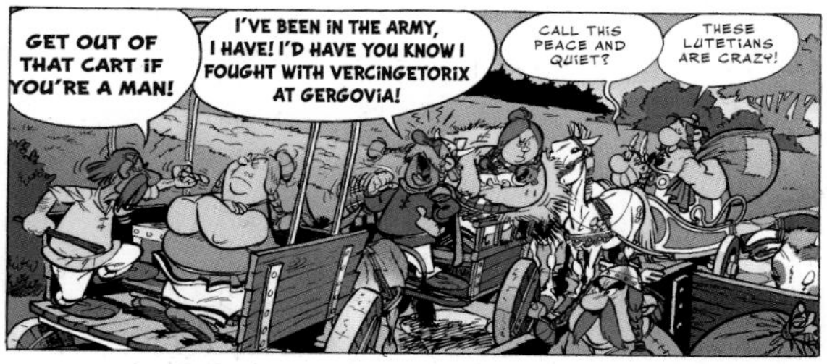
GET OUT OF THAT CART IF YOU'RE A MAN!
I'VE BEEN IN THE ARMY, I HAVE! I'D HAVE YOU KNOW I FOUGHT WITH VERCINGETORIX AT GERGOVIA!
CALL THIS PEACE AND QUIET?
THESE LUTETIANS ARE CRAZY!

It's not unusual to see what ought to have been a pleasant excursion degenerate into a pitched battle, leading to amphora-necks and tailbacks paralysing the traffic for millia and millia passuum.

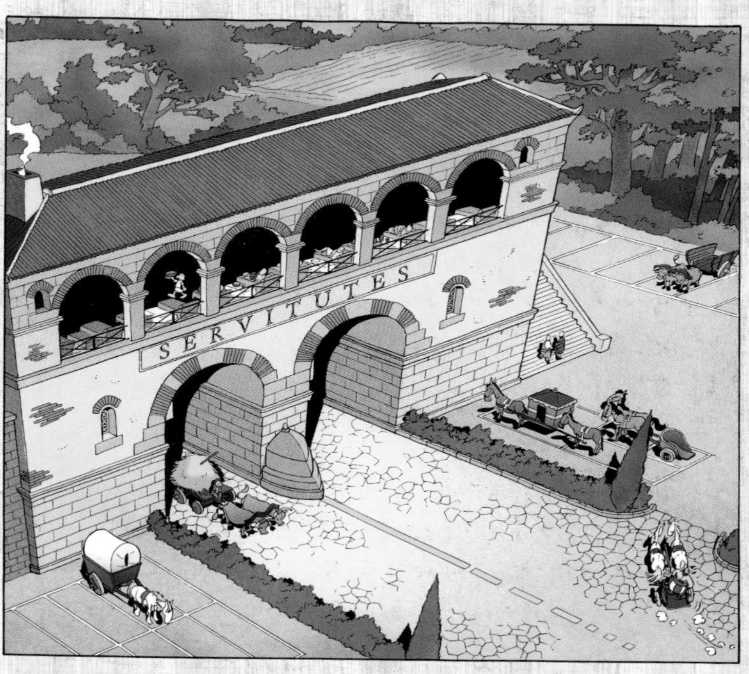
SERVITUTES

# ROMAN ROADS GUARANTEED C% FOR ALL MOD CONS

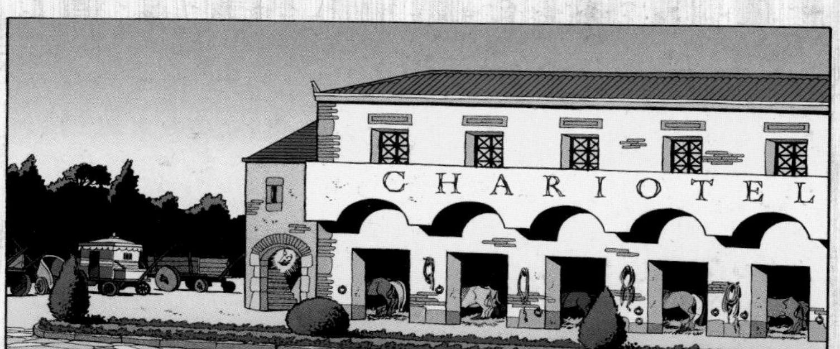
CHARIOTEL

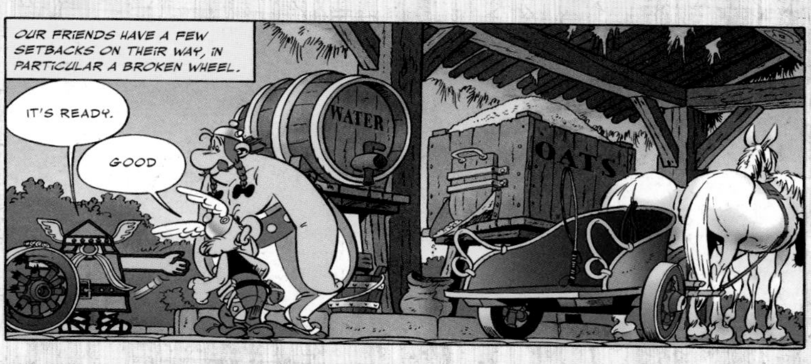
OUR FRIENDS HAVE A FEW SETBACKS ON THEIR WAY, IN PARTICULAR A BROKEN WHEEL.
IT'S READY.
GOOD
WATER
OATS

*With servitutes, chariotels and service stations along the way, every effort has been made to provide for the comfort of chariot drivers!*

Frames from *Asterix and the Banquet* and *Asterix in Switzerland*

1 – About 4.5 kph  2 – Turnip eaten instead of potatoes  3 – Latin, slow coach

And there's one thing the Gauls will never understand: it's not a good idea to eat a heavy meal at lunchtime when you still have some way to travel. But we Gauls are greedy pigs, we feed our faces with wild boar, and we can't resist one last hornful of Aquitanian wine to wash it down! In spite of the marble slabs up beside the roads telling us not to drink and drive,we forget that the amphora can kill as easily as an enemy soldier's pilum. Remember:

"One amphora, fine!
Two amphorae, watch out!"

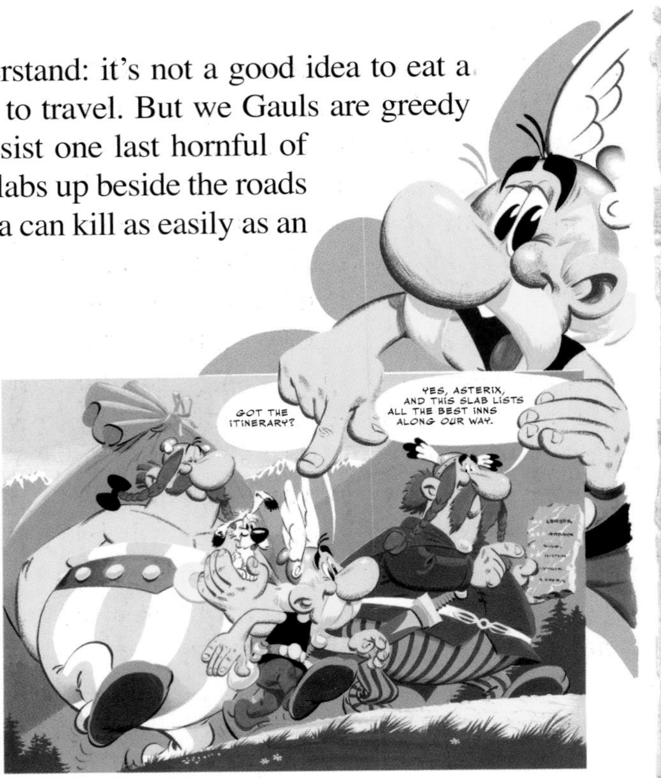

GOT THE ITINERARY?
YES, ASTERIX, AND THIS SLAB LISTS ALL THE BEST INNS ALONG OUR WAY.


Almost everyone has his own chariot these days, but how many people are really good drivers? How many of you know, for instance, what distance you need to stop a galloping horse? XX feet! A pair of oxen going full speed ahead will need XXX feet to come to a halt! And if you are travelling by litter, it takes X feet for slaves carrying you at full tilt to pull up.

Furthermore, whether you're in a Roman chariot, an ox cart or a litter, sports-chariot driving is best left to the professional aurigae. Allow me to offer a little advice: you're not Ben Hur. Controlled skids and sharp bends taken at the gallop are not for you. You have a good chariot, you're proud of the power under its yoke, but use that power only to keep yourself out of danger.

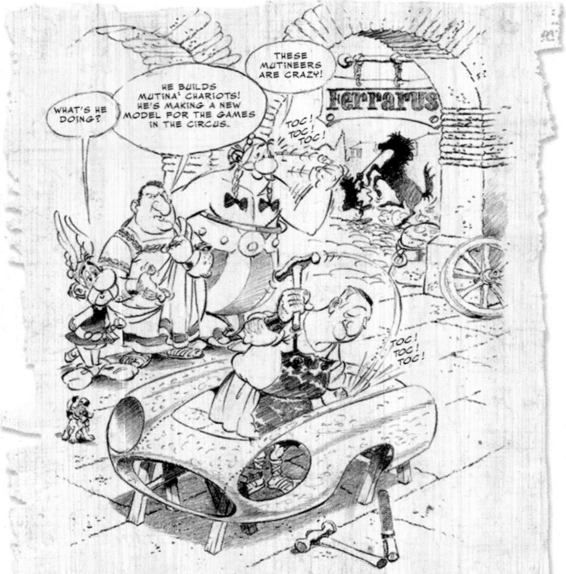

WHAT'S HE DOING?
HE BUILDS MUTINA[1] CHARIOTS! HE'S MAKING A NEW MODEL FOR THE GAMES IN THE CIRCUS.
THESE MUTINEERS ARE CRAZY!
Ferrarus
TOC! TOC! TOC!
TOC! TOC! TOC!


*For professional aurigae, a visit to the Ferrarus chariot-building factory is a great event.*

Another problem with our roads is that too few service stations are open at night. If you break down after sunset, I suppose you could always try looking for a veterinary surgeon, but you'll be told, "I'm here to sell hay, not doctor the draught animals." In addition, getting spare parts is difficult. If one of your team of oxen needs replacing, you'll be told that the spare part has to come from Charolais, and you may spend your whole holiday waiting for your ox to arrive. Because even when it gets into its stride an ox doesn't move fast!

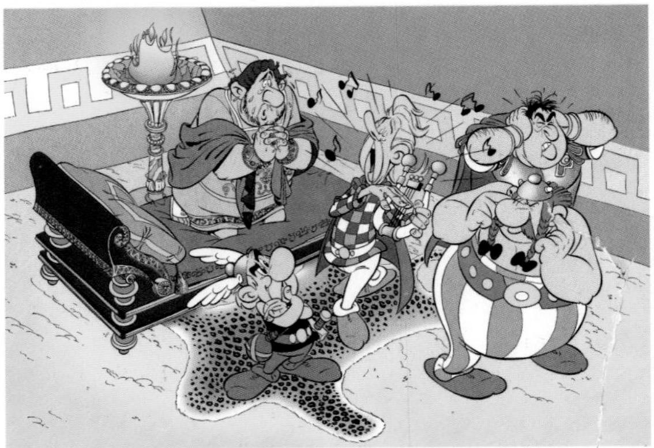

*To be sure of a warm welcome everywhere, take your travelling bard with you.*

1 – Present-day Modena

There are also the inns along your way. It's better not to stop on the off chance, because you may have a nasty surprise when the bill arrives, and your wallet could suffer a sizeable catapult-hole. Of course, if you like fancy cooking you'll find luxury establishments rated by golden sickles in the specialist guides, places where you can eat pâté of ants' thighs, stuffed nightingale tongues and candied trout-heads. But if you prefer simple fare, stop at one of the places with transport carts parked outside. You'll find a friendly atmosphere where they serve you good roast boar, chilled barley beer, and hydromel like Mater makes it.

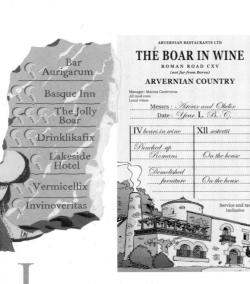

Bar Aurigarum
Basque Inn
The Jolly Boar
Drinklikafix
Lakeside Hotel
Vermicellix
Invinoveritas

ARVERNIAN RESTAURANTS LTD

THE BOAR IN WINE

ROMAN ROAD CXV

*(not far from Borvo)*

ARVERNIAN COUNTRY

Manager: Marcus Carniverus
All mod cons
Local wines

Messrs : *Astérix and Obelix*

Date : *Year* L *B.-C.*

| | |
|---|---|
| IV *boars in wine* | XII *sestertii* |
| *Punched-up Romans* | *On the house* |
| *Demolished furniture* | *On the house* |

Service and tax inclusive

If you want a place to stay on your way, it's best to reserve in advance, or you may have to sleep the night in your chariot. Many like to go camping, but then you should follow the example of the Romans: never forget to dig a ditch and put up a fence around your tent. That will keep out attacking barbarians, who are sometimes a nuisance and spoil your good night's sleep.

Finally, I must add that only prudent Gauls enjoy their travels, but I wish all of you happy holidays!

Text by René Goscinny published in *Pilote*, no. 347, 16 June 1966.

# HOLIDAY IDEAS

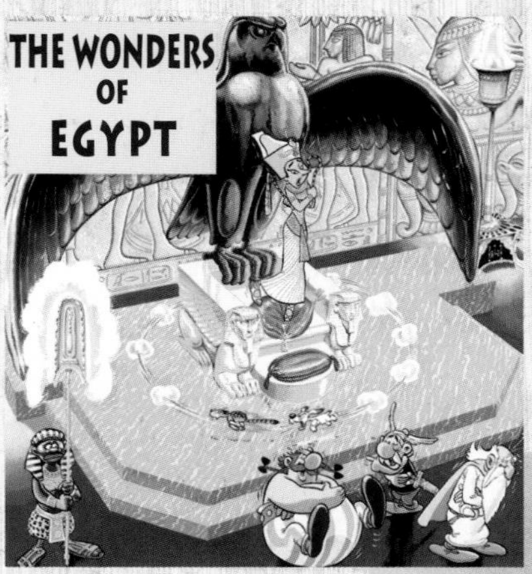

THE WONDERS OF EGYPT


*Egypt and its queen of queens. Nothing but happy memories for the Gauls. We're not so sure about Cleopatra ...*

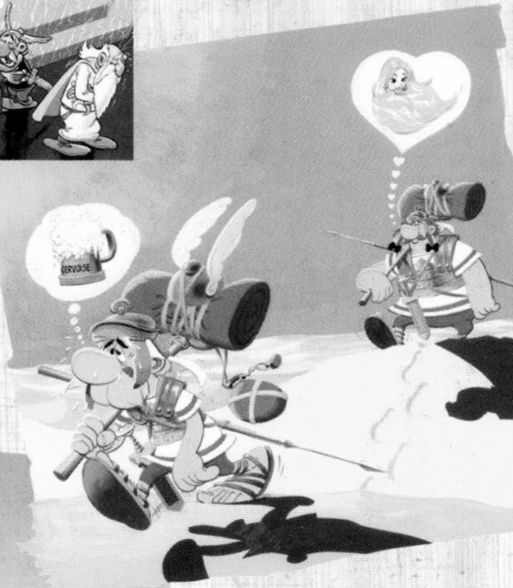

*Adventurers at heart will enjoy a stay in the middle of the desert. An unexpected encounter with your deepest longings!*

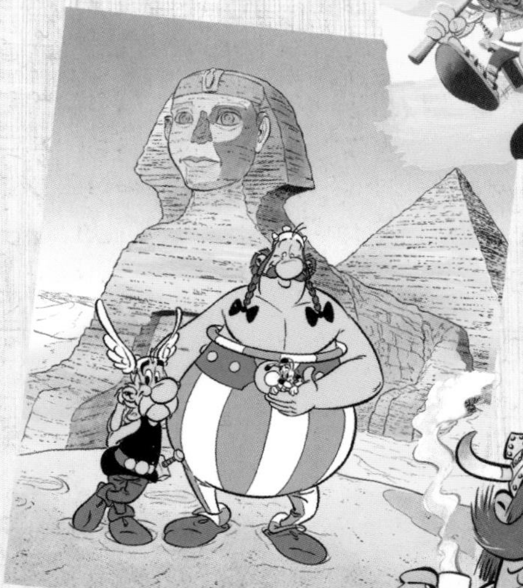

*To impress your friends, have souvenir pictures carved in front of historic monuments.*

BRETAGNE
MARE BRITANNICUM
GAVLE


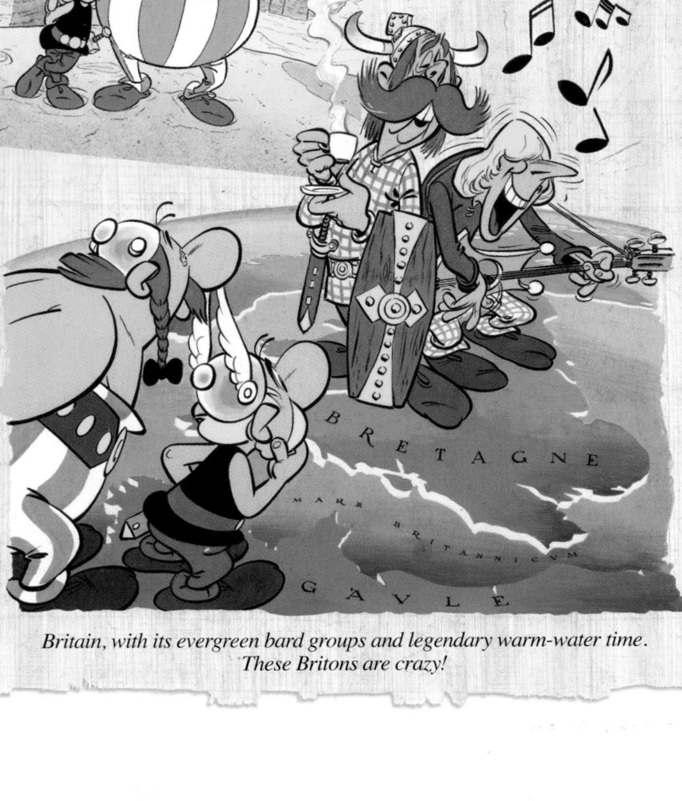

*Britain, with its evergreen bard groups and legendary warm-water time. These Britons are crazy!*

# PUT YOUR TRAVELS ON THE MAP

**Useful accessories to take, souvenirs from foreign lands: everything you need for going away in times of classical antiquity.**

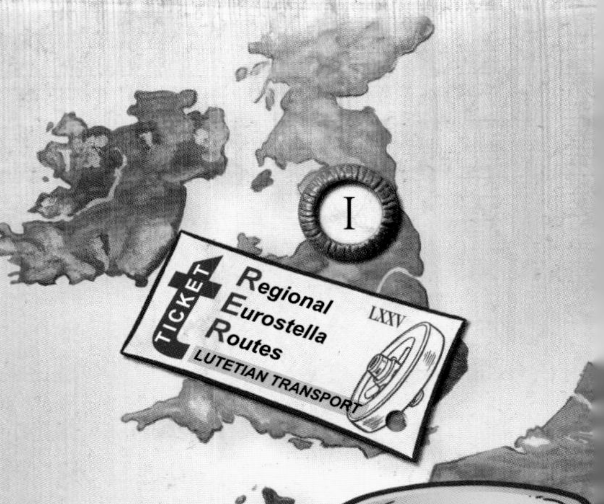

I
TICKET
Regional
Eurostella
Routes
LXXV
LUTETIAN TRANSPORT


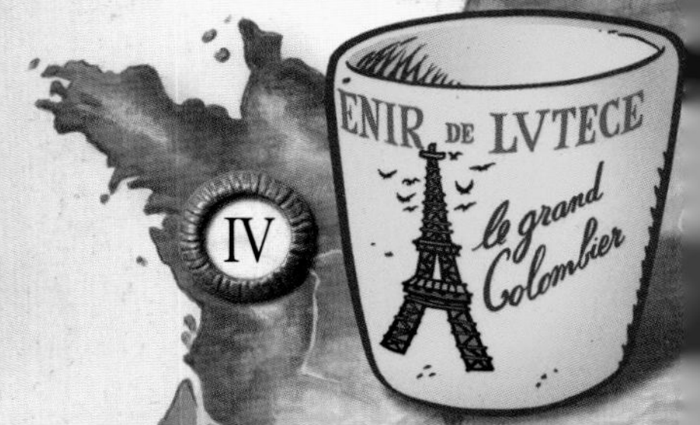

IV
ENIR DE LVTECE
le grand Colombier


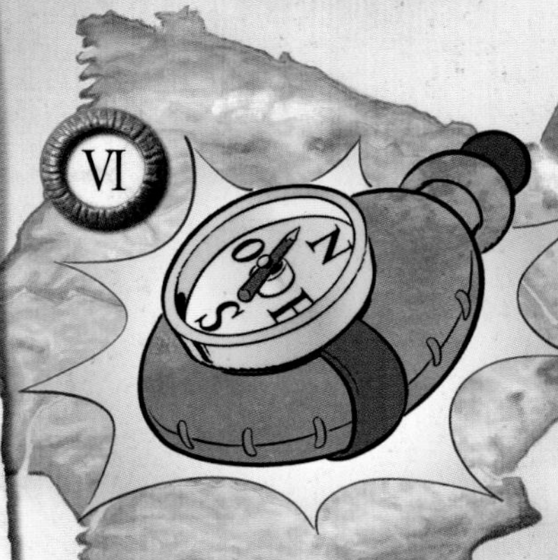

VI
N
S
E
O


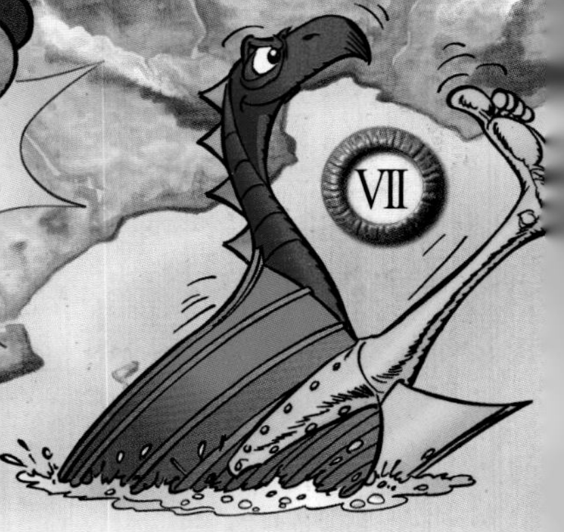

VII


**I.**
**Ticket for the Regional Eurostella Routes**
public chariot company.

**II.**
**Set of Viking drinking skulls,**
great fun for merry evenings at home with friends!

**III.**
**Postcard slabs.**
To keep in touch with your loved ones.

**IV.**
**Souvenir of the greatest city in the universe.**

**V.**
**Travel guide,**
to make sure you don't miss anything!

**VI.**
**Gourd of NSP.**
Don't lose your bearings!
This gourd of North Star potion will help you find them again any time.
Exclusively brewed by Viking magicians.

**VII.**
**Shipwrecked galley.**
Do you enjoy sport?
Prepare to board a pirate ship (optional)

**VIII.**
**A few sestertii.**
Collectors: keep the loose change from every province.
Egyptian talents are the most sought after.

**IX.**
**Club Middle Sea brochure slab.**
Lots of leisure activities in idyllic surroundings.

**X.**
**Pyramid paperweight.**
The Great Pyramid in the snow.
You dream of it, the Egyptians make it!

**XI.**
**Passport.**
Issued by the Imperial authorities.
You will need one of these to move freely around all the countries that are part of the Pax Romana.

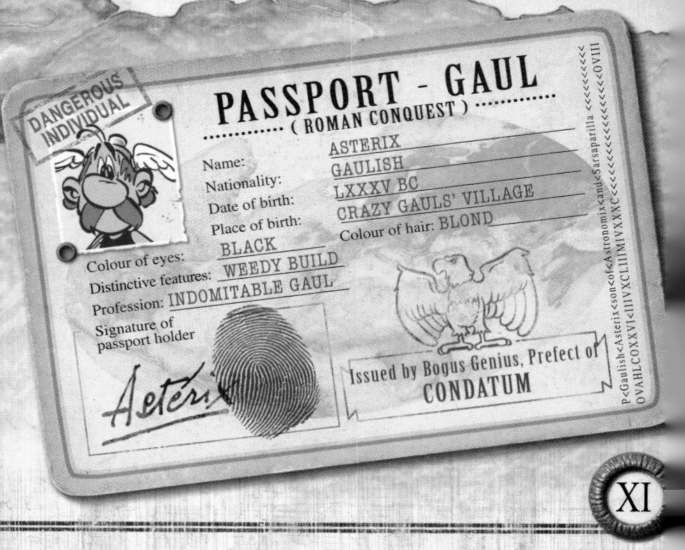

DANGEROUS INDIVIDUAL
PASSPORT - GAUL
( ROMAN CONQUEST )
Name: ASTERIX
Nationality: GAULISH
Date of birth: LXXXV BC
Place of birth: CRAZY GAULS' VILLAGE
Colour of hair: BLOND
Colour of eyes: BLACK
Distinctive features: WEEDY BUILD
Profession: INDOMITABLE GAUL
Signature of passport holder
Asterix
Issued by Bogus Genius, Prefect of CONDATUM
P<Gaulish<Asterix<son<of<Astronomix<and<Sarsaparilla<<<<<<<<<<<<
OVAHLCOXXVI<IIIVXCLIIIMIVXXC<<<<<<<<<<<<<<OVIII
XI

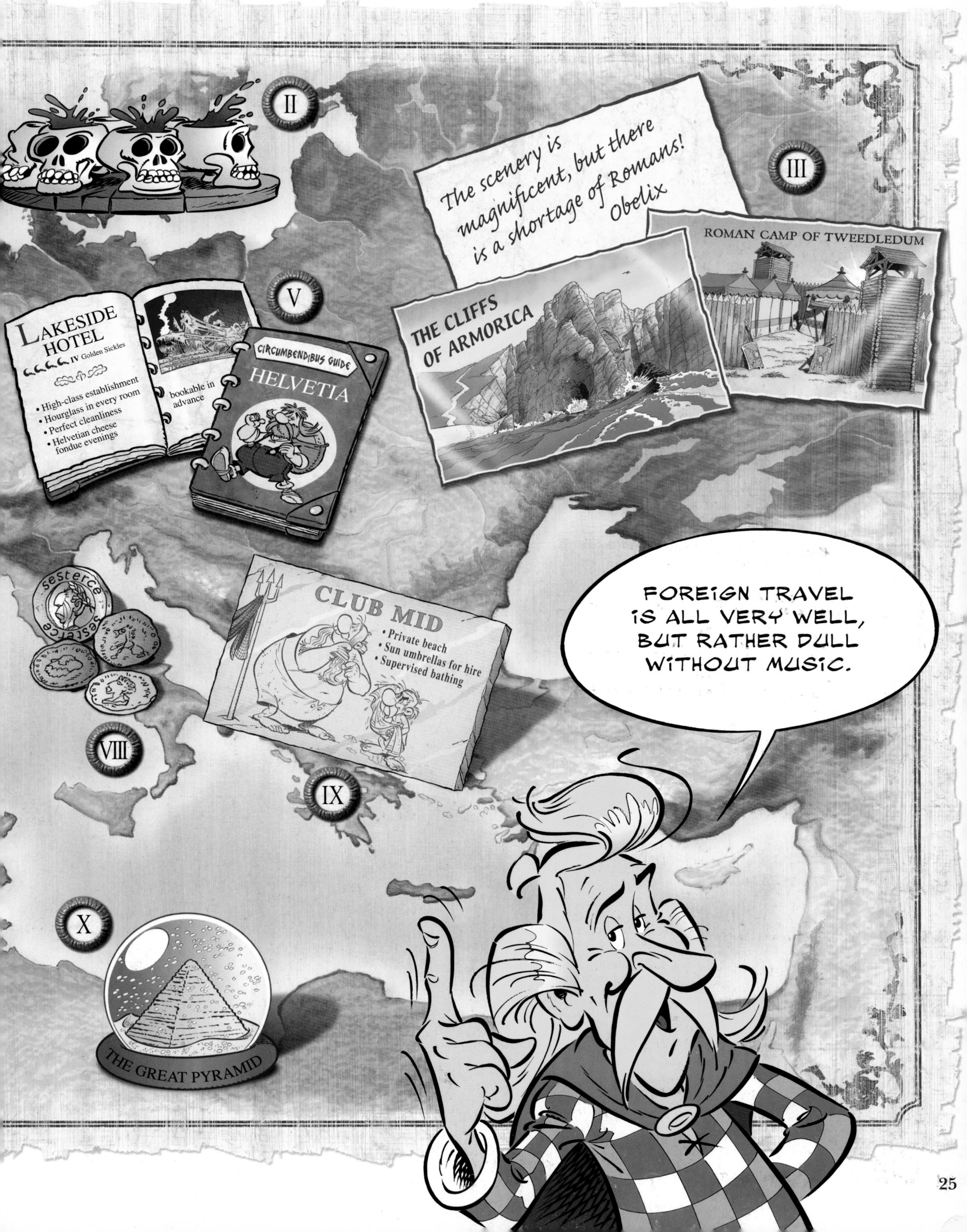
II
III
V
VIII
IX
X
The scenery is magnificent, but there is a shortage of Romans! Obelix
ROMAN CAMP OF TWEEDLEDUM
THE CLIFFS OF ARMORICA
LAKESIDE HOTEL
IV Golden Sickles
• High-class establishment
• Hourglass in every room
• Perfect cleanliness
• Helvetian cheese fondue evenings
bookable in advance
CIRCUMBENDIBUS GUIDE
HELVETIA
sesterce
CLUB MID
• Private beach
• Sun umbrellas for hire
• Supervised bathing
THE GREAT PYRAMID
FOREIGN TRAVEL IS ALL VERY WELL, BUT RATHER DULL WITHOUT MUSIC.

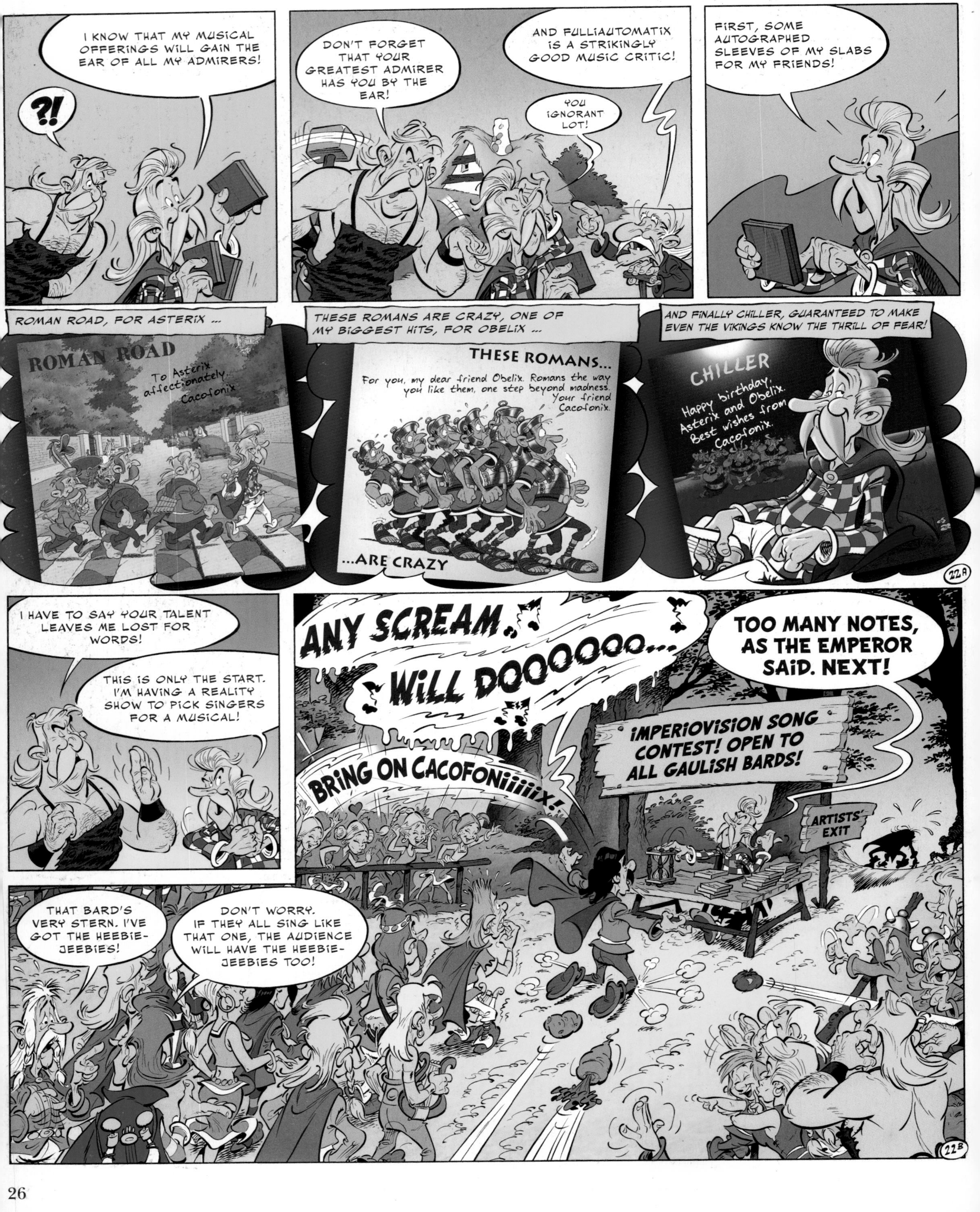
I KNOW THAT MY MUSICAL OFFERINGS WILL GAIN THE EAR OF ALL MY ADMIRERS!
?!
DON'T FORGET THAT YOUR GREATEST ADMIRER HAS YOU BY THE EAR!
AND FULLIAUTOMATIX IS A STRIKINGLY GOOD MUSIC CRITIC!
YOU IGNORANT LOT!
FIRST, SOME AUTOGRAPHED SLEEVES OF MY SLABS FOR MY FRIENDS!
ROMAN ROAD, FOR ASTERIX ...
ROMAN ROAD
To Asterix affectionately. Cacofonix
THESE ROMANS ARE CRAZY, ONE OF MY BIGGEST HITS, FOR OBELIX ...
THESE ROMANS...
For you, my dear friend Obelix. Romans the way you like them, one step beyond madness. Your friend Cacofonix.
...ARE CRAZY
AND FINALLY CHILLER, GUARANTEED TO MAKE EVEN THE VIKINGS KNOW THE THRILL OF FEAR!
CHILLER
Happy birthday, Asterix and Obelix. Best wishes from Cacofonix.
22A
I HAVE TO SAY YOUR TALENT LEAVES ME LOST FOR WORDS!
THIS IS ONLY THE START. I'M HAVING A REALITY SHOW TO PICK SINGERS FOR A MUSICAL!
ANY SCREAM... WILL DOOOOOO...
TOO MANY NOTES, AS THE EMPEROR SAID. NEXT!
IMPERIOVISION SONG CONTEST! OPEN TO ALL GAULISH BARDS!
BRING ON CACOFONIiiiiiX!
ARTISTS' EXIT
THAT BARD'S VERY STERN. I'VE GOT THE HEEBIE-JEEBIES!
DON'T WORRY. IF THEY ALL SING LIKE THAT ONE, THE AUDIENCE WILL HAVE THE HEEBIE-JEEBIES TOO!
22B

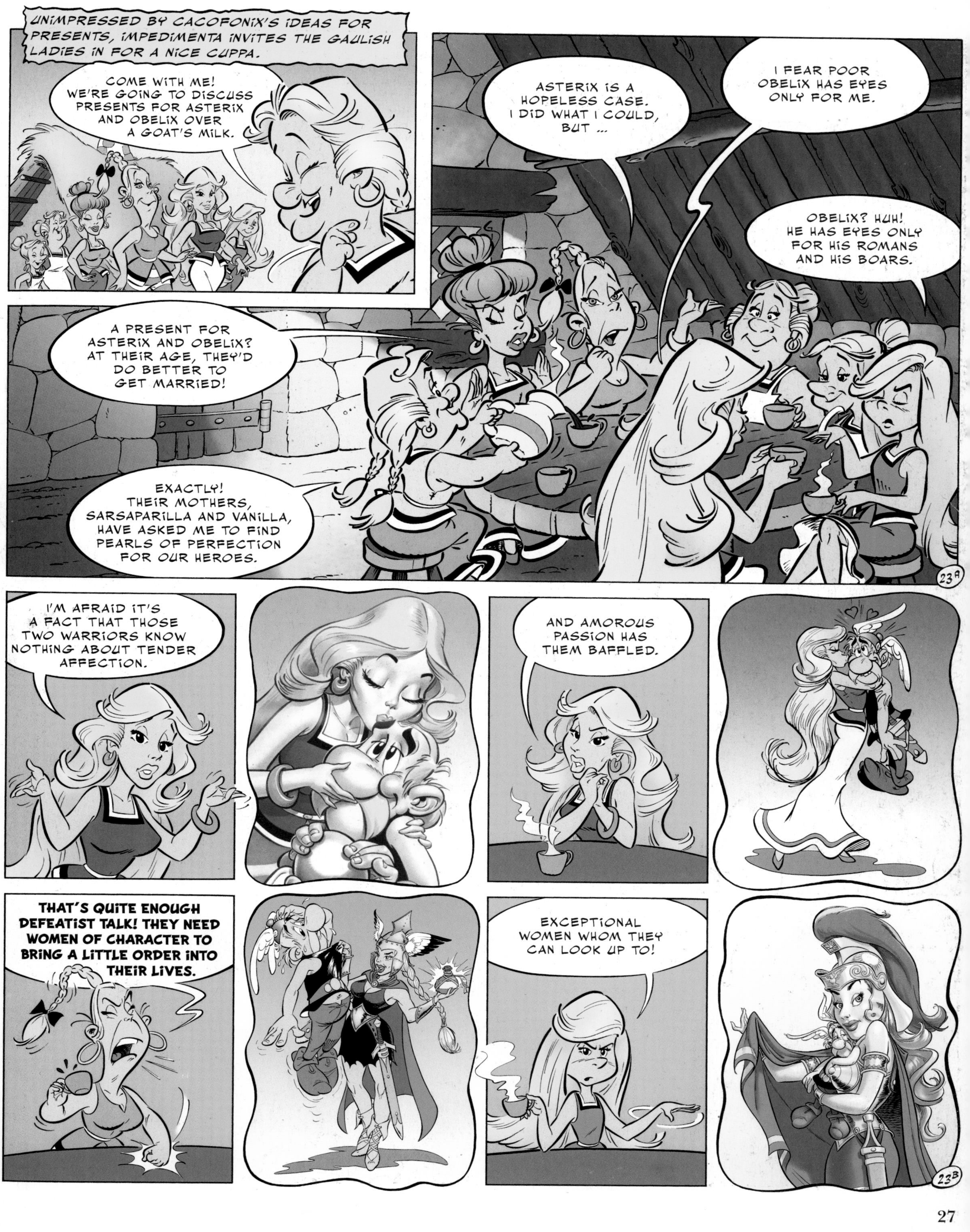
UNIMPRESSED BY CACOFONIX'S IDEAS FOR PRESENTS, IMPEDIMENTA INVITES THE GAULISH LADIES IN FOR A NICE CUPPA.
COME WITH ME! WE'RE GOING TO DISCUSS PRESENTS FOR ASTERIX AND OBELIX OVER A GOAT'S MILK.
ASTERIX IS A HOPELESS CASE. I DID WHAT I COULD, BUT ...
I FEAR POOR OBELIX HAS EYES ONLY FOR ME.
OBELIX? HUH! HE HAS EYES ONLY FOR HIS ROMANS AND HIS BOARS.
A PRESENT FOR ASTERIX AND OBELIX? AT THEIR AGE, THEY'D DO BETTER TO GET MARRIED!
EXACTLY! THEIR MOTHERS, SARSAPARILLA AND VANILLA, HAVE ASKED ME TO FIND PEARLS OF PERFECTION FOR OUR HEROES.
23A
I'M AFRAID IT'S A FACT THAT THOSE TWO WARRIORS KNOW NOTHING ABOUT TENDER AFFECTION.
AND AMOROUS PASSION HAS THEM BAFFLED.
THAT'S QUITE ENOUGH DEFEATIST TALK! THEY NEED WOMEN OF CHARACTER TO BRING A LITTLE ORDER INTO THEIR LIVES.
EXCEPTIONAL WOMEN WHOM THEY CAN LOOK UP TO!
23B

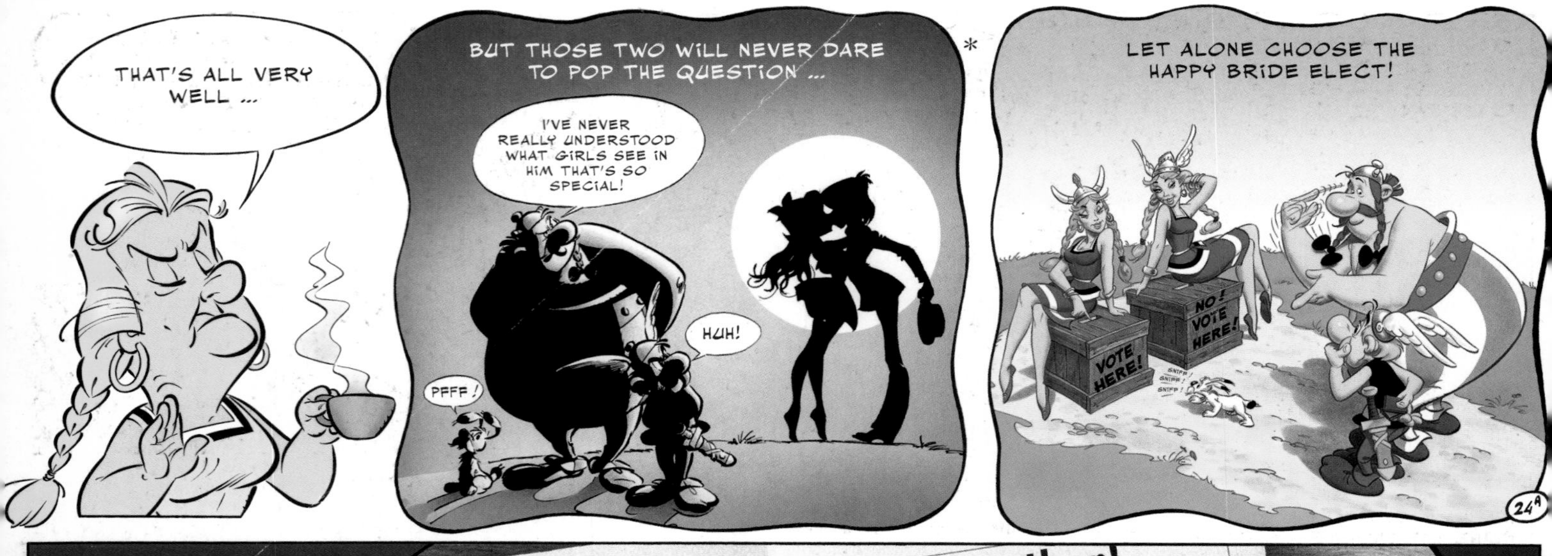
THAT'S ALL VERY WELL ...
BUT THOSE TWO WILL NEVER DARE TO POP THE QUESTION ...
I'VE NEVER REALLY UNDERSTOOD WHAT GIRLS SEE IN HIM THAT'S SO SPECIAL!
HUH!
PFFF!
*
LET ALONE CHOOSE THE HAPPY BRIDE ELECT!
VOTE HERE!
NO! VOTE HERE!
24A

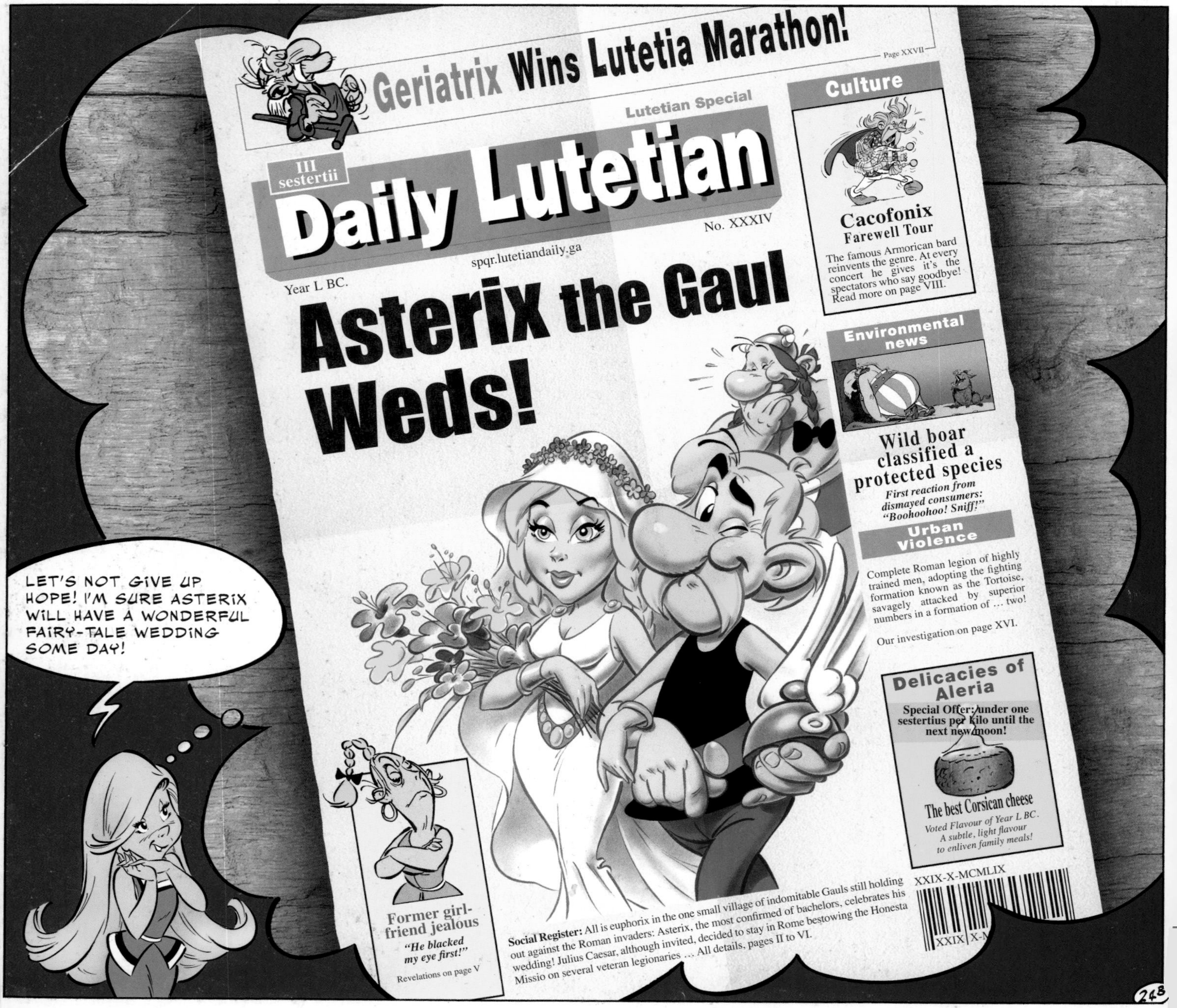
Geriatrix Wins Lutetia Marathon!
Page XXVII
Lutetian Special
III sestertii
Daily Lutetian
No. XXXIV
spqr.lutetiandaily.ga
Year L BC.
Asterix the Gaul Weds!
Culture
Cacofonix Farewell Tour
The famous Armorican bard reinvents the genre. At every concert he gives it's the spectators who say goodbye! Read more on page VIII.
Environmental news
Wild boar classified a protected species
First reaction from dismayed consumers: "Boohoohoo! Sniff!"
Urban Violence
Complete Roman legion of highly trained men, adopting the fighting formation known as the Tortoise, savagely attacked by superior numbers in a formation of … two!
Our investigation on page XVI.
Delicacies of Aleria
Special Offer: under one sestertius per kilo until the next new moon!
The best Corsican cheese
Voted Flavour of Year L BC. A subtle, light flavour to enliven family meals!
XXIX-X-MCMLIX
Former girl-friend jealous
"He blacked my eye first!"
Revelations on page V
Social Register: All is euphorix in the one small village of indomitable Gauls still holding out against the Roman invaders: Asterix, the most confirmed of bachelors, celebrates his wedding! Julius Caesar, although invited, decided to stay in Rome bestowing the Honesta Missio on several veteran legionaries … All details, pages II to VI.
LET'S NOT GIVE UP HOPE! I'M SURE ASTERIX WILL HAVE A WONDERFUL FAIRY-TALE WEDDING SOME DAY!
24B

* A tribute to Dany. Dany, real name Daniel Henrotin, is a Belgian strip cartoon artist. The silhouette shows one of his characters.

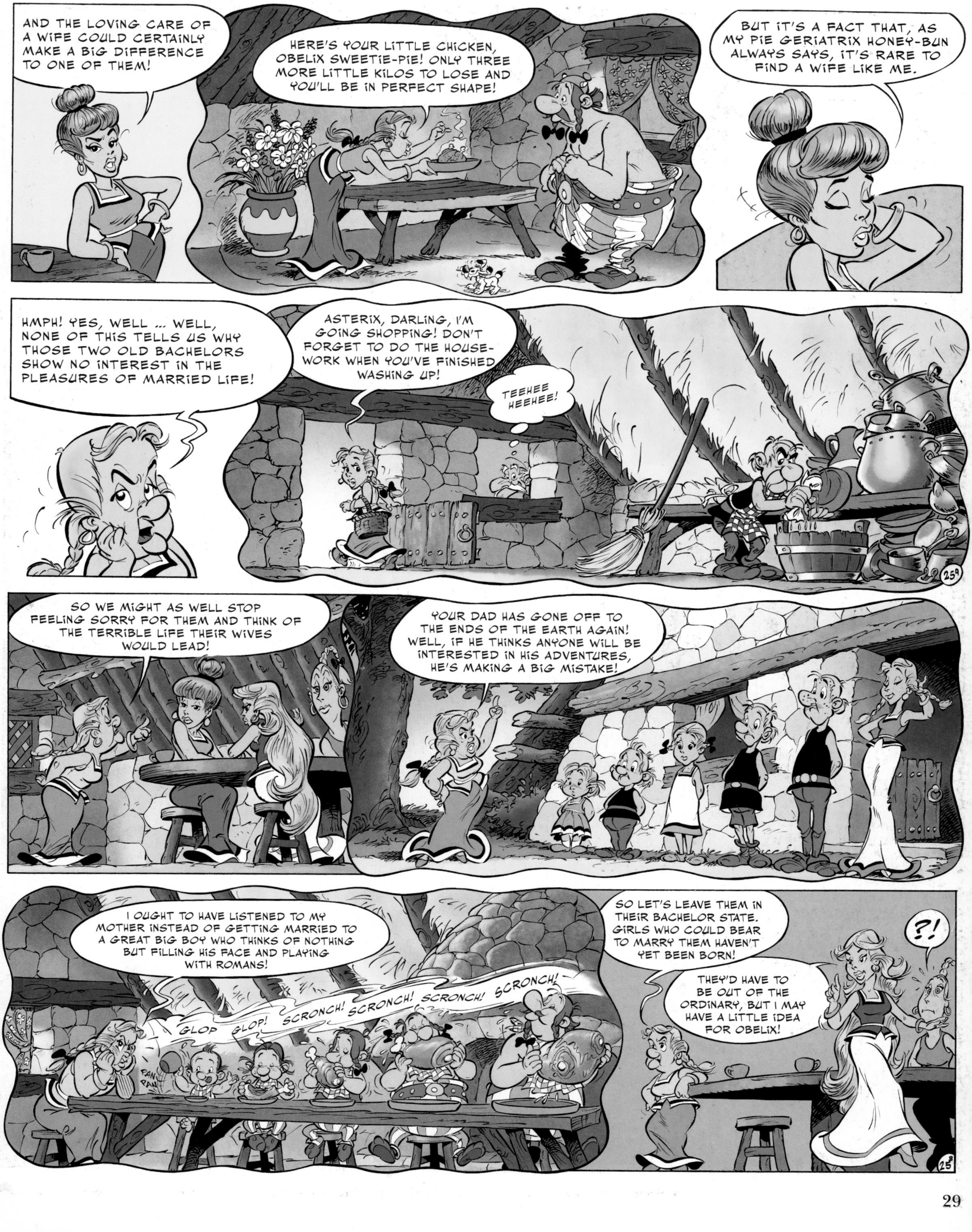
AND THE LOVING CARE OF A WIFE COULD CERTAINLY MAKE A BIG DIFFERENCE TO ONE OF THEM!
HERE'S YOUR LITTLE CHICKEN, OBELIX SWEETIE-PIE! ONLY THREE MORE LITTLE KILOS TO LOSE AND YOU'LL BE IN PERFECT SHAPE!
BUT IT'S A FACT THAT, AS MY PIE GERIATRIX HONEY-BUN ALWAYS SAYS, IT'S RARE TO FIND A WIFE LIKE ME.
HMPH! YES, WELL ... WELL, NONE OF THIS TELLS US WHY THOSE TWO OLD BACHELORS SHOW NO INTEREST IN THE PLEASURES OF MARRIED LIFE!
ASTERIX, DARLING, I'M GOING SHOPPING! DON'T FORGET TO DO THE HOUSE-WORK WHEN YOU'VE FINISHED WASHING UP!
TEEHEE HEEHEE!
SO WE MIGHT AS WELL STOP FEELING SORRY FOR THEM AND THINK OF THE TERRIBLE LIFE THEIR WIVES WOULD LEAD!
YOUR DAD HAS GONE OFF TO THE ENDS OF THE EARTH AGAIN! WELL, IF HE THINKS ANYONE WILL BE INTERESTED IN HIS ADVENTURES, HE'S MAKING A BIG MISTAKE!
I OUGHT TO HAVE LISTENED TO MY MOTHER INSTEAD OF GETTING MARRIED TO A GREAT BIG BOY WHO THINKS OF NOTHING BUT FILLING HIS FACE AND PLAYING WITH ROMANS!
GLOP GLOP! SCRONCH! SCRONCH! SCRONCH! SCRONCH!
FAN PAN
SO LET'S LEAVE THEM IN THEIR BACHELOR STATE. GIRLS WHO COULD BEAR TO MARRY THEM HAVEN'T YET BEEN BORN!
?!
THEY'D HAVE TO BE OUT OF THE ORDINARY, BUT I MAY HAVE A LITTLE IDEA FOR OBELIX!

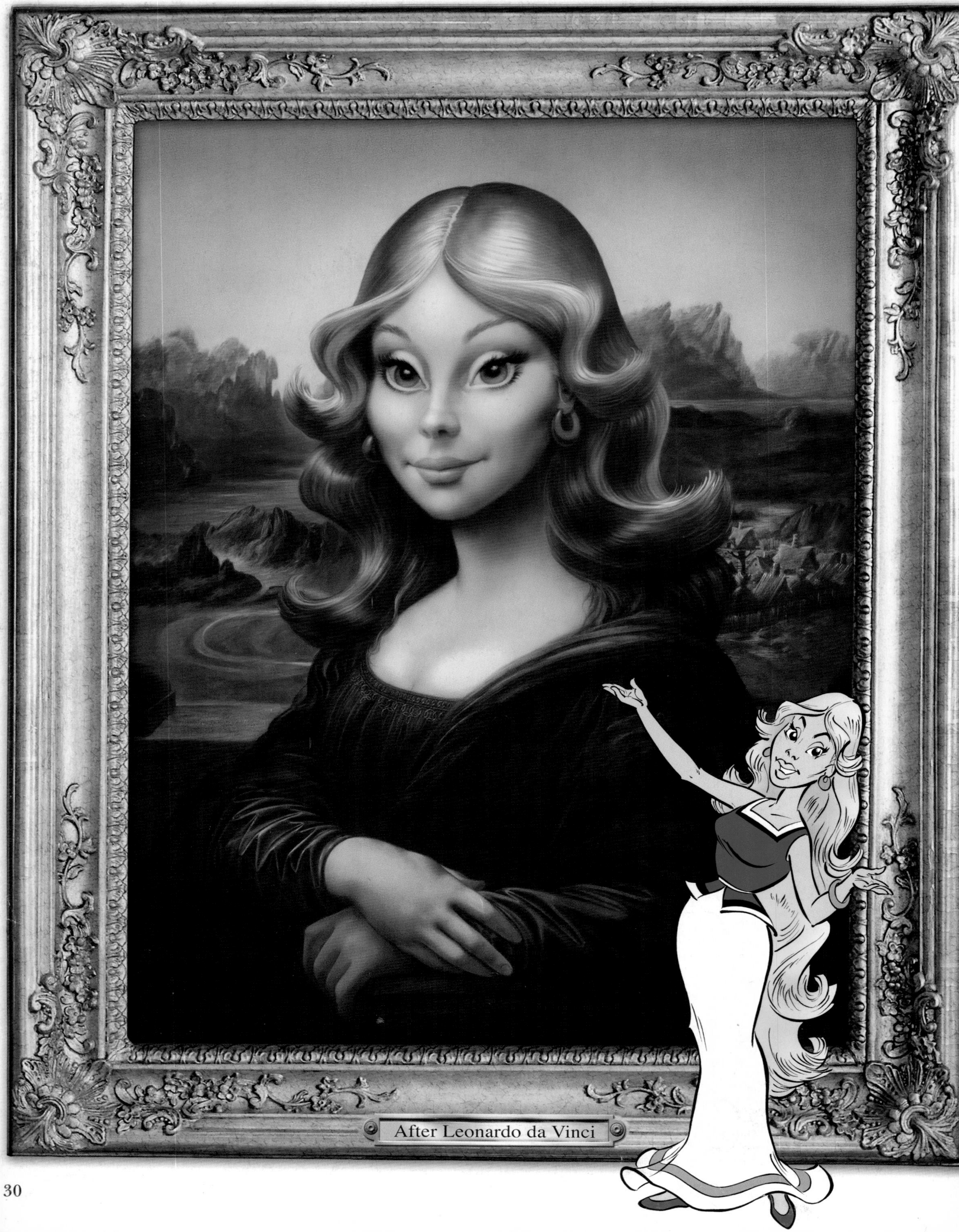
After Leonardo da Vinci

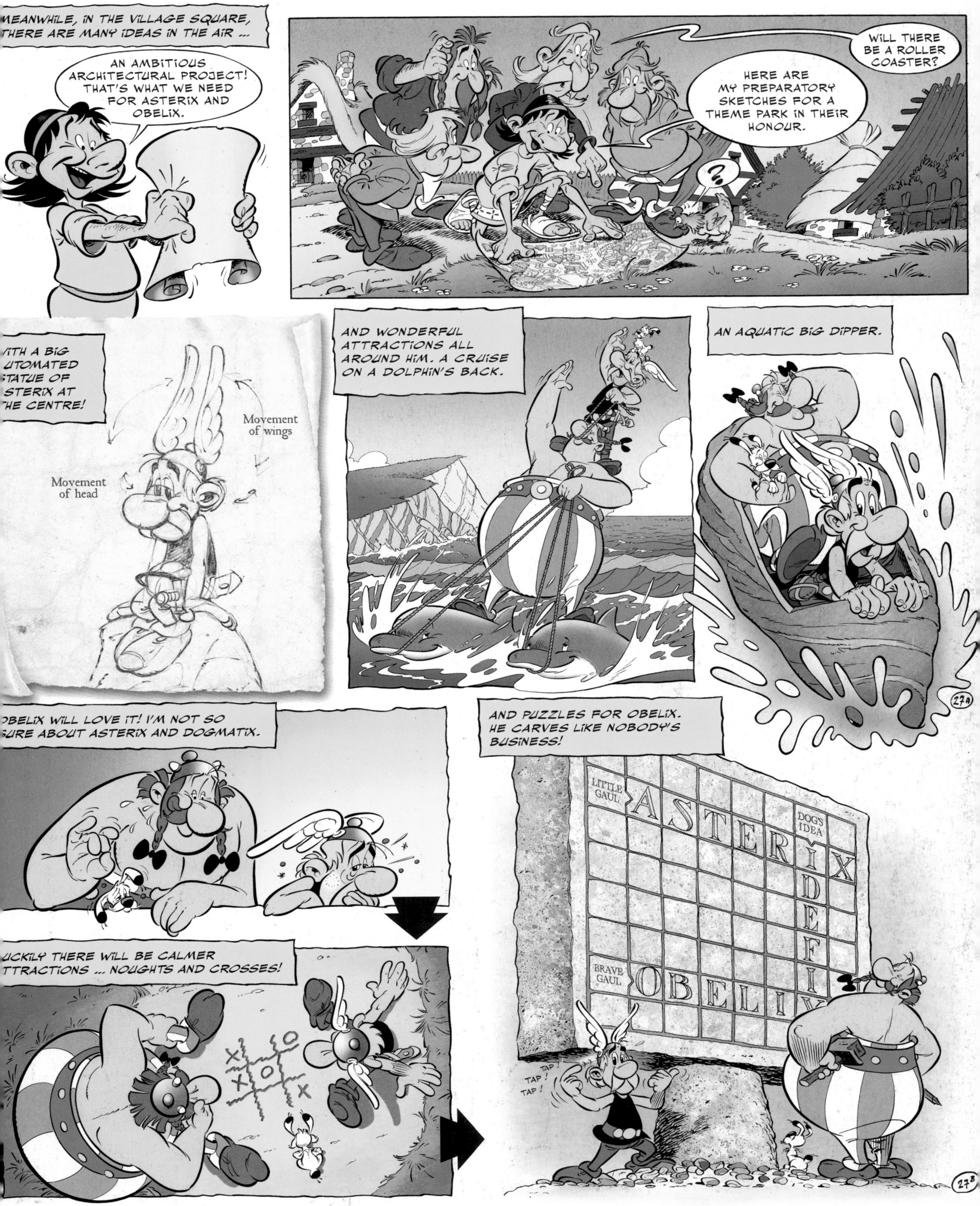

MEANWHILE, IN THE VILLAGE SQUARE, THERE ARE MANY IDEAS IN THE AIR ...
AN AMBITIOUS ARCHITECTURAL PROJECT! THAT'S WHAT WE NEED FOR ASTERIX AND OBELIX.
HERE ARE MY PREPARATORY SKETCHES FOR A THEME PARK IN THEIR HONOUR.
WILL THERE BE A ROLLER COASTER?
?
WITH A BIG AUTOMATED STATUE OF ASTERIX AT THE CENTRE!
Movement of wings
Movement of head
AND WONDERFUL ATTRACTIONS ALL AROUND HIM. A CRUISE ON A DOLPHIN'S BACK.
AN AQUATIC BIG DIPPER.
27A
OBELIX WILL LOVE IT! I'M NOT SO SURE ABOUT ASTERIX AND DOGMATIX.
LUCKILY THERE WILL BE CALMER ATTRACTIONS ... NOUGHTS AND CROSSES!
AND PUZZLES FOR OBELIX. HE CARVES LIKE NOBODY'S BUSINESS!
LITTLE GAUL
ASTERIX
DOG'S IDEA
IDEFIX
BRAVE GAUL
OBELIX
TAP! TAP! TAP!
27B

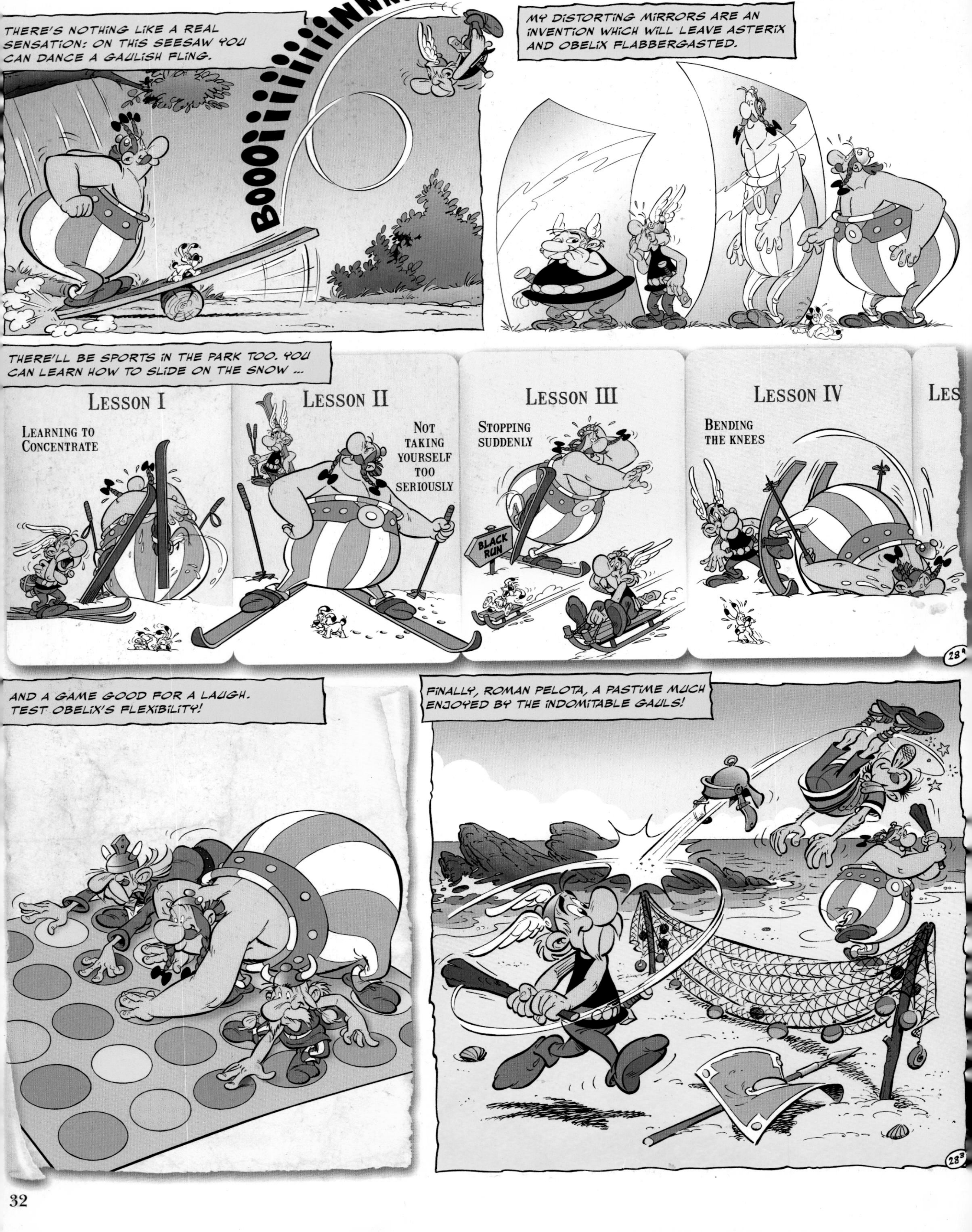
THERE'S NOTHING LIKE A REAL SENSATION: ON THIS SEESAW YOU CAN DANCE A GAULISH FLING.
BOOOIIIIIIIIINNNGG...
MY DISTORTING MIRRORS ARE AN INVENTION WHICH WILL LEAVE ASTERIX AND OBELIX FLABBERGASTED.
THERE'LL BE SPORTS IN THE PARK TOO. YOU CAN LEARN HOW TO SLIDE ON THE SNOW ...
LESSON I
LEARNING TO CONCENTRATE
LESSON II
NOT TAKING YOURSELF TOO SERIOUSLY
LESSON III
STOPPING SUDDENLY
BLACK RUN
LESSON IV
BENDING THE KNEES
AND A GAME GOOD FOR A LAUGH. TEST OBELIX'S FLEXIBILITY!
FINALLY, ROMAN PELOTA, A PASTIME MUCH ENJOYED BY THE INDOMITABLE GAULS!

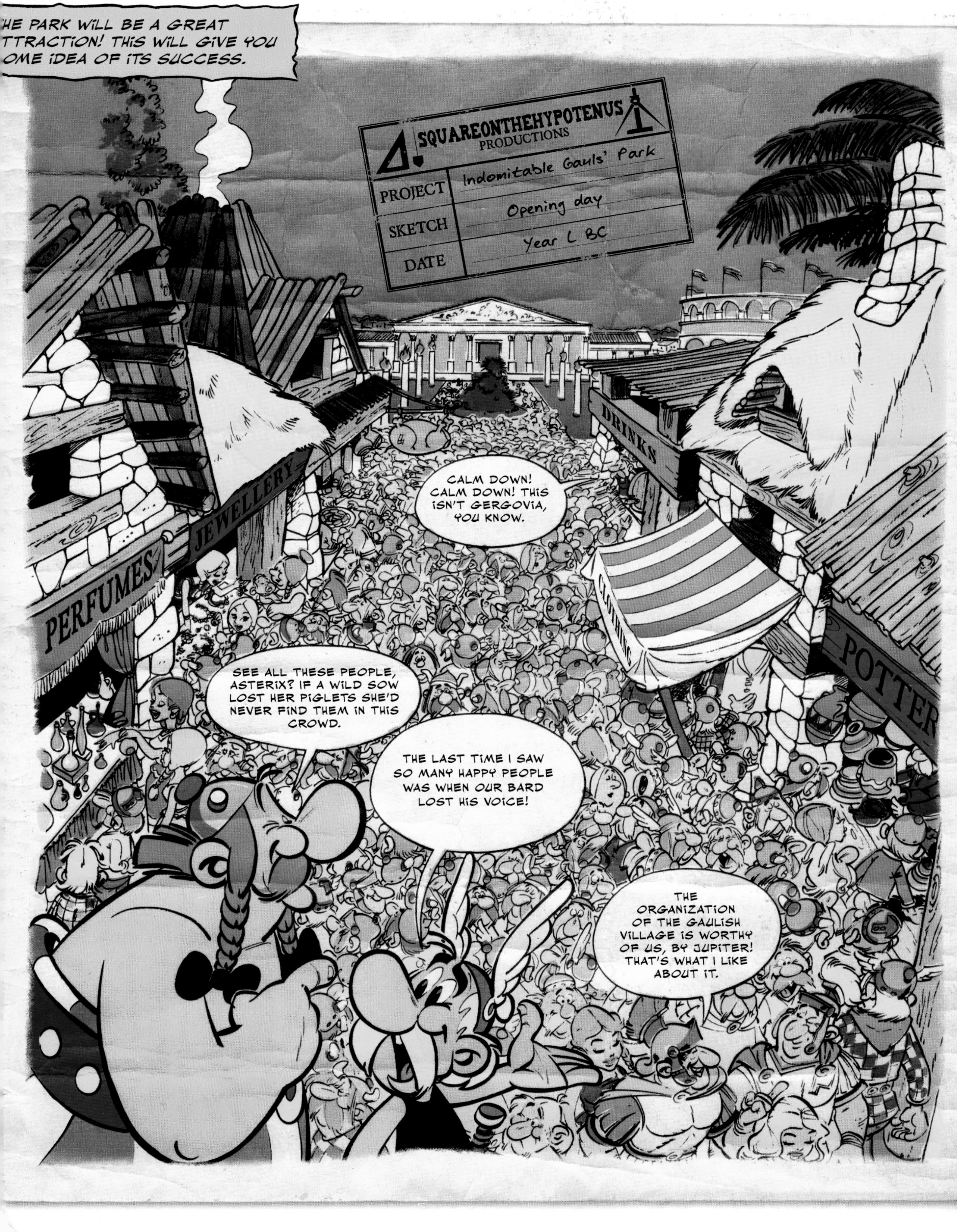
HE PARK WILL BE A GREAT TTRACTION! THIS WILL GIVE YOU OME IDEA OF ITS SUCCESS.
SQUAREONTHEHYPOTENUS PRODUCTIONS
PROJECT Indomitable Gauls' Park
SKETCH Opening day
DATE Year L BC
DRINKS
JEWELLERY
PERFUMES
CLOTHING
POTTER
CALM DOWN! CALM DOWN! THIS ISN'T GERGOVIA, YOU KNOW.
SEE ALL THESE PEOPLE, ASTERIX? IF A WILD SOW LOST HER PIGLETS SHE'D NEVER FIND THEM IN THIS CROWD.
THE LAST TIME I SAW SO MANY HAPPY PEOPLE WAS WHEN OUR BARD LOST HIS VOICE!
THE ORGANIZATION OF THE GAULISH VILLAGE IS WORTHY OF US, BY JUPITER! THAT'S WHAT I LIKE ABOUT IT.

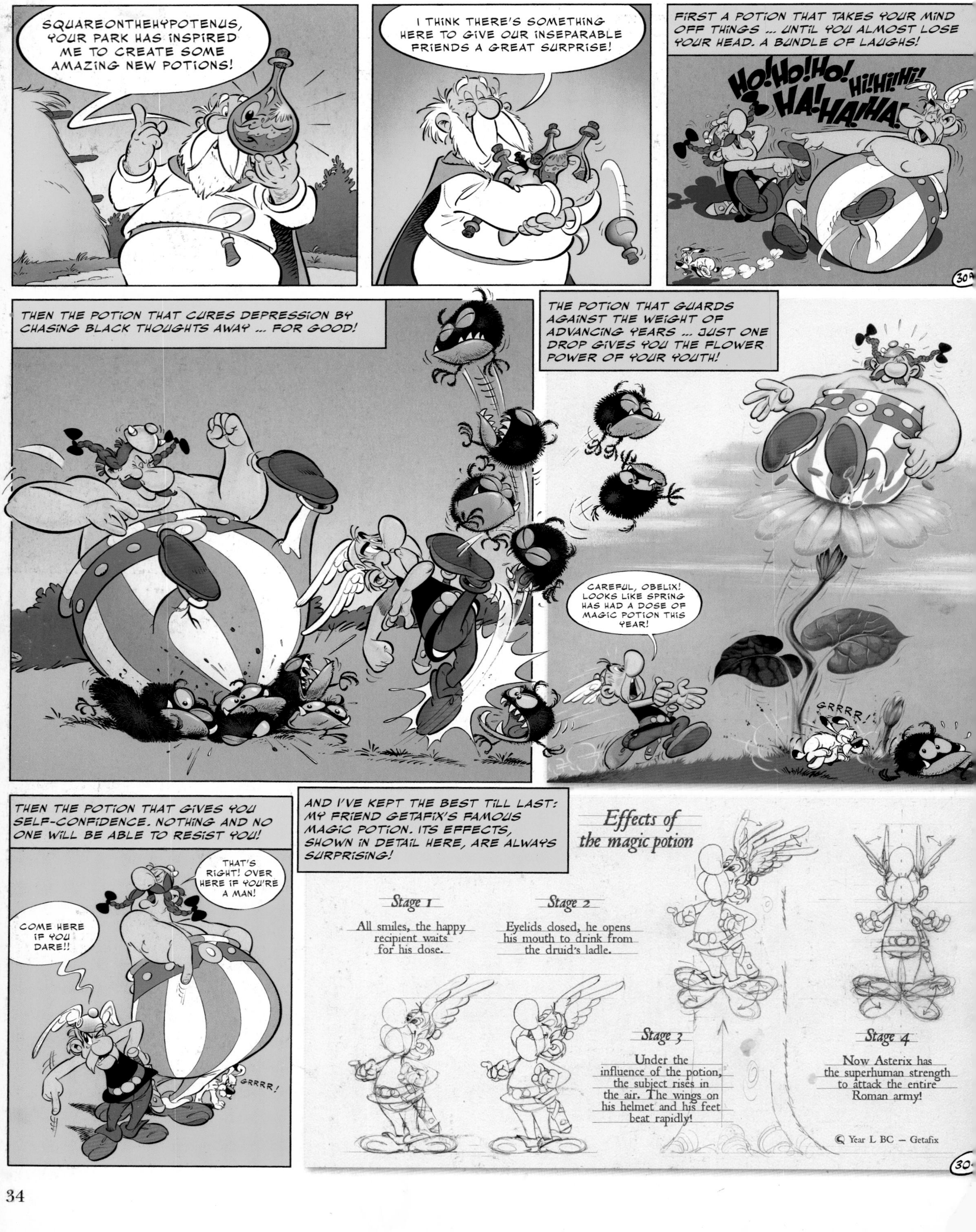
SQUAREONTHEHYPOTENUS, YOUR PARK HAS INSPIRED ME TO CREATE SOME AMAZING NEW POTIONS!
I THINK THERE'S SOMETHING HERE TO GIVE OUR INSEPARABLE FRIENDS A GREAT SURPRISE!
FIRST A POTION THAT TAKES YOUR MIND OFF THINGS ... UNTIL YOU ALMOST LOSE YOUR HEAD. A BUNDLE OF LAUGHS!
HO!HO!HO! HI!HI!HI! HA!HA!HA!
THEN THE POTION THAT CURES DEPRESSION BY CHASING BLACK THOUGHTS AWAY ... FOR GOOD!
THE POTION THAT GUARDS AGAINST THE WEIGHT OF ADVANCING YEARS ... JUST ONE DROP GIVES YOU THE FLOWER POWER OF YOUR YOUTH!
CAREFUL, OBELIX! LOOKS LIKE SPRING HAS HAD A DOSE OF MAGIC POTION THIS YEAR!
GRRRRR!
THEN THE POTION THAT GIVES YOU SELF-CONFIDENCE. NOTHING AND NO ONE WILL BE ABLE TO RESIST YOU!
THAT'S RIGHT! OVER HERE IF YOU'RE A MAN!
COME HERE IF YOU DARE!!
GRRRR!
AND I'VE KEPT THE BEST TILL LAST: MY FRIEND GETAFIX'S FAMOUS MAGIC POTION. ITS EFFECTS, SHOWN IN DETAIL HERE, ARE ALWAYS SURPRISING!
Effects of the magic potion
Stage 1
All smiles, the happy recipient waits for his dose.
Stage 2
Eyelids closed, he opens his mouth to drink from the druid's ladle.
Stage 3
Under the influence of the potion, the subject rises in the air. The wings on his helmet and his feet beat rapidly!
Stage 4
Now Asterix has the superhuman strength to attack the entire Roman army!
© Year L BC – Getafix

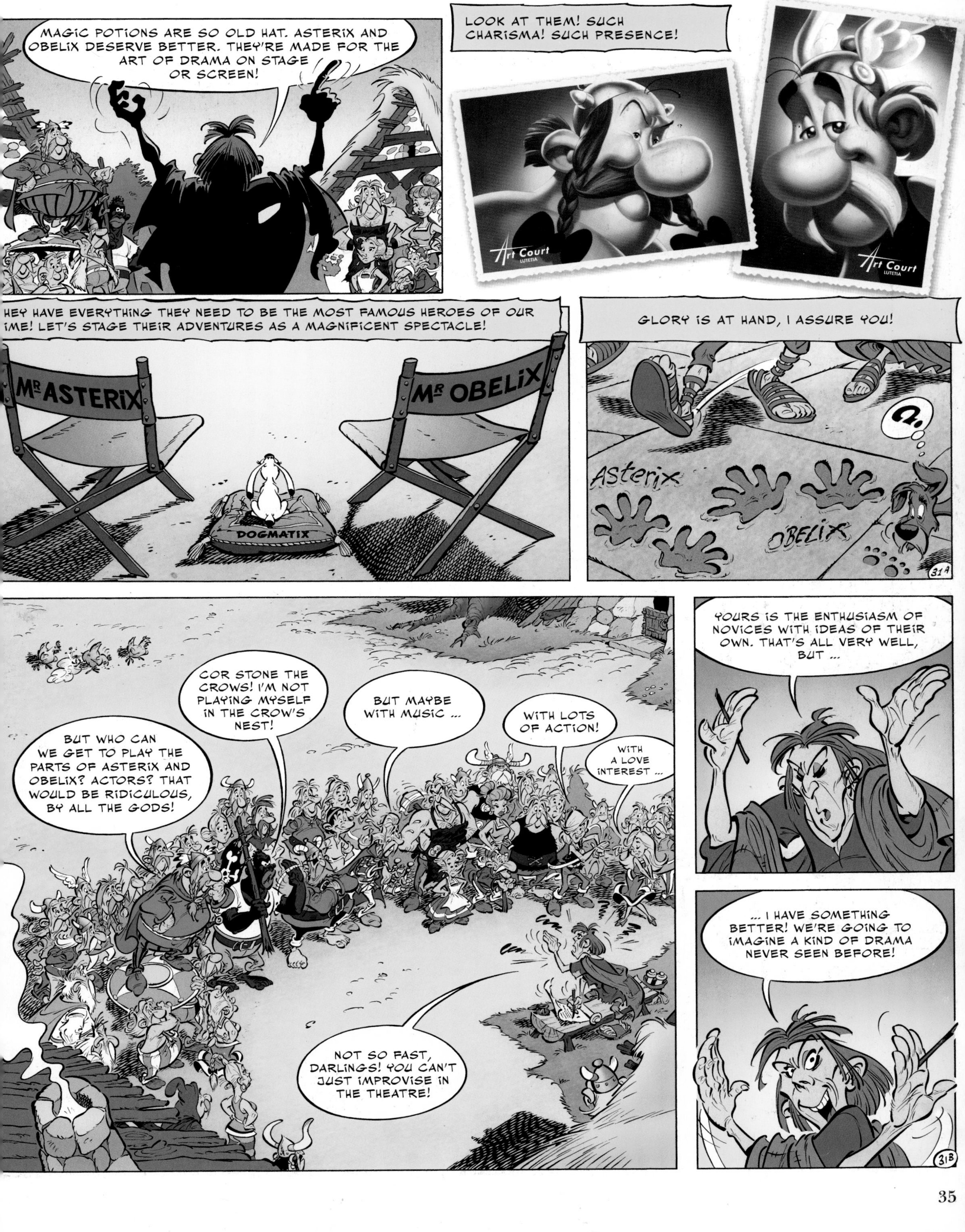
MAGIC POTIONS ARE SO OLD HAT. ASTERIX AND OBELIX DESERVE BETTER. THEY'RE MADE FOR THE ART OF DRAMA ON STAGE OR SCREEN!
LOOK AT THEM! SUCH CHARISMA! SUCH PRESENCE!
Art Court LUTETIA
Art Court LUTETIA
HEY HAVE EVERYTHING THEY NEED TO BE THE MOST FAMOUS HEROES OF OUR IME! LET'S STAGE THEIR ADVENTURES AS A MAGNIFICENT SPECTACLE!
MR ASTERIX
MR OBELIX
DOGMATIX
GLORY IS AT HAND, I ASSURE YOU!
Asterix
OBELIX
31A
BUT WHO CAN WE GET TO PLAY THE PARTS OF ASTERIX AND OBELIX? ACTORS? THAT WOULD BE RIDICULOUS, BY ALL THE GODS!
COR STONE THE CROWS! I'M NOT PLAYING MYSELF IN THE CROW'S NEST!
BUT MAYBE WITH MUSIC ...
WITH LOTS OF ACTION!
WITH A LOVE INTEREST ...
NOT SO FAST, DARLINGS! YOU CAN'T JUST IMPROVISE IN THE THEATRE!
YOURS IS THE ENTHUSIASM OF NOVICES WITH IDEAS OF THEIR OWN. THAT'S ALL VERY WELL, BUT ...
... I HAVE SOMETHING BETTER! WE'RE GOING TO IMAGINE A KIND OF DRAMA NEVER SEEN BEFORE!
31B

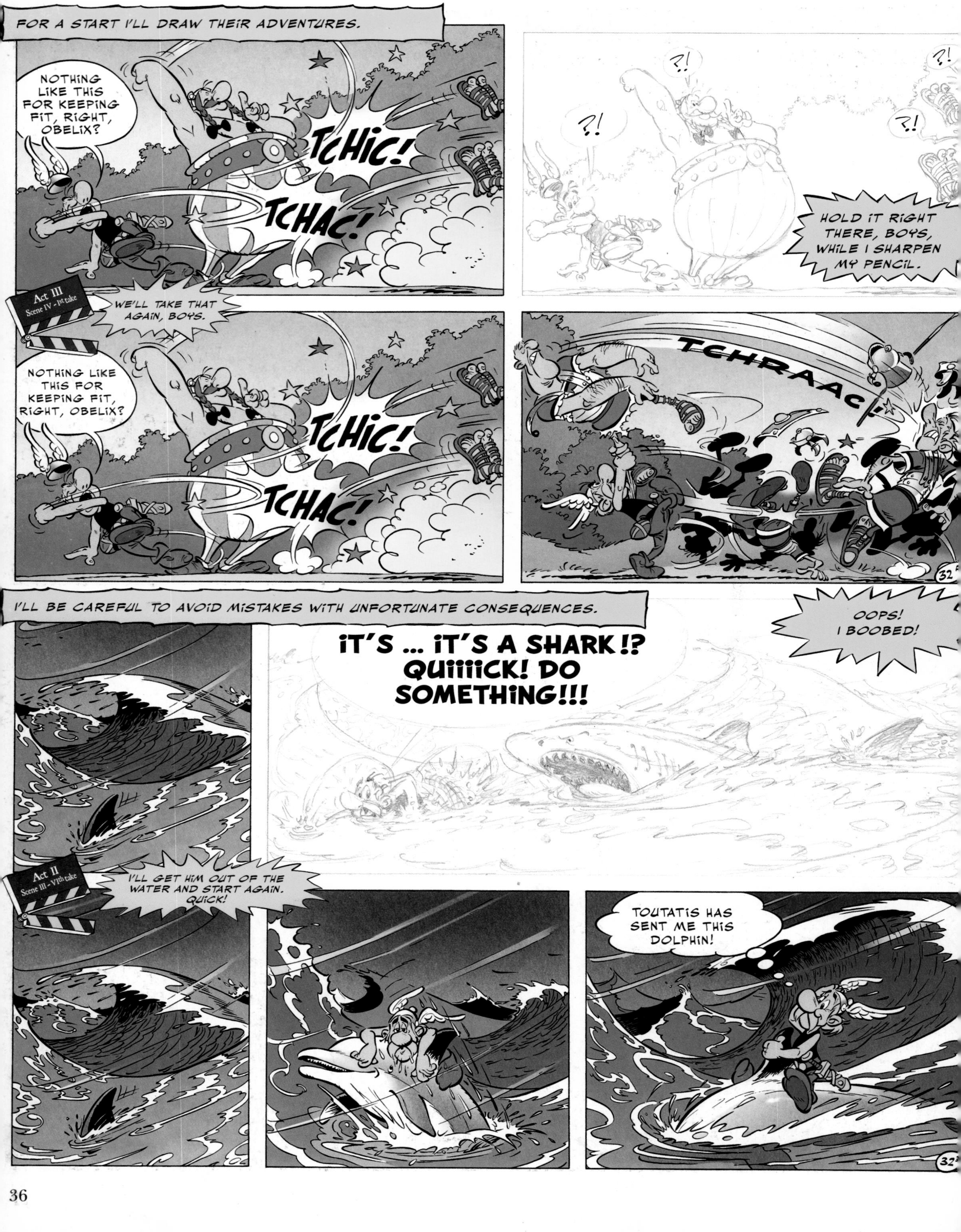
FOR A START I'LL DRAW THEIR ADVENTURES.
NOTHING LIKE THIS FOR KEEPING FIT, RIGHT, OBELIX?
TCHIC!
TCHAC!
?!
?!
?!
?!
HOLD IT RIGHT THERE, BOYS, WHILE I SHARPEN MY PENCIL.
Act III Scene IV - 1st take
WE'LL TAKE THAT AGAIN, BOYS.
NOTHING LIKE THIS FOR KEEPING FIT, RIGHT, OBELIX?
TCHIC!
TCHAC!
TCHRAAAC!
I'LL BE CAREFUL TO AVOID MISTAKES WITH UNFORTUNATE CONSEQUENCES.
IT'S ... IT'S A SHARK!? QUIIIICK! DO SOMETHING!!!
OOPS! I BOOBED!
Act II Scene III - Vth take
I'LL GET HIM OUT OF THE WATER AND START AGAIN. QUICK!
TOUTATIS HAS SENT ME THIS DOLPHIN!

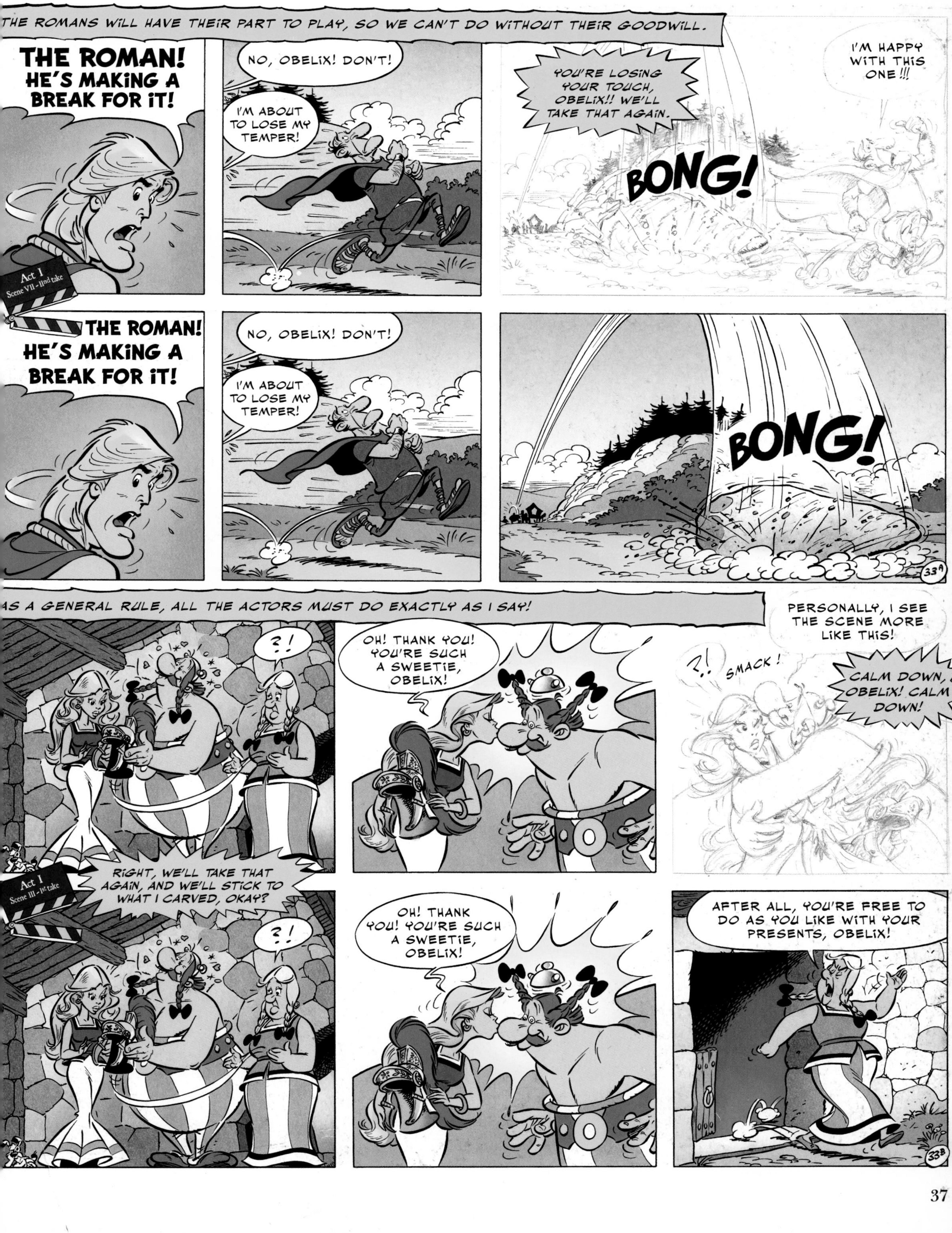

THE ROMANS WILL HAVE THEIR PART TO PLAY, SO WE CAN'T DO WITHOUT THEIR GOODWILL.
THE ROMAN! HE'S MAKING A BREAK FOR IT!
Act 1 Scene VII - IInd take
NO, OBELIX! DON'T!
I'M ABOUT TO LOSE MY TEMPER!
YOU'RE LOSING YOUR TOUCH, OBELIX!! WE'LL TAKE THAT AGAIN.
BONG!
I'M HAPPY WITH THIS ONE!!!
THE ROMAN! HE'S MAKING A BREAK FOR IT!
NO, OBELIX! DON'T!
I'M ABOUT TO LOSE MY TEMPER!
BONG!
339
AS A GENERAL RULE, ALL THE ACTORS MUST DO EXACTLY AS I SAY!
?!
OH! THANK YOU! YOU'RE SUCH A SWEETIE, OBELIX!
PERSONALLY, I SEE THE SCENE MORE LIKE THIS!
?!
SMACK!
CALM DOWN, OBELIX! CALM DOWN!
Act 1 Scene III - 1st take
RIGHT, WE'LL TAKE THAT AGAIN, AND WE'LL STICK TO WHAT I CARVED, OKAY?
?!
OH! THANK YOU! YOU'RE SUCH A SWEETIE, OBELIX!
AFTER ALL, YOU'RE FREE TO DO AS YOU LIKE WITH YOUR PRESENTS, OBELIX!
338

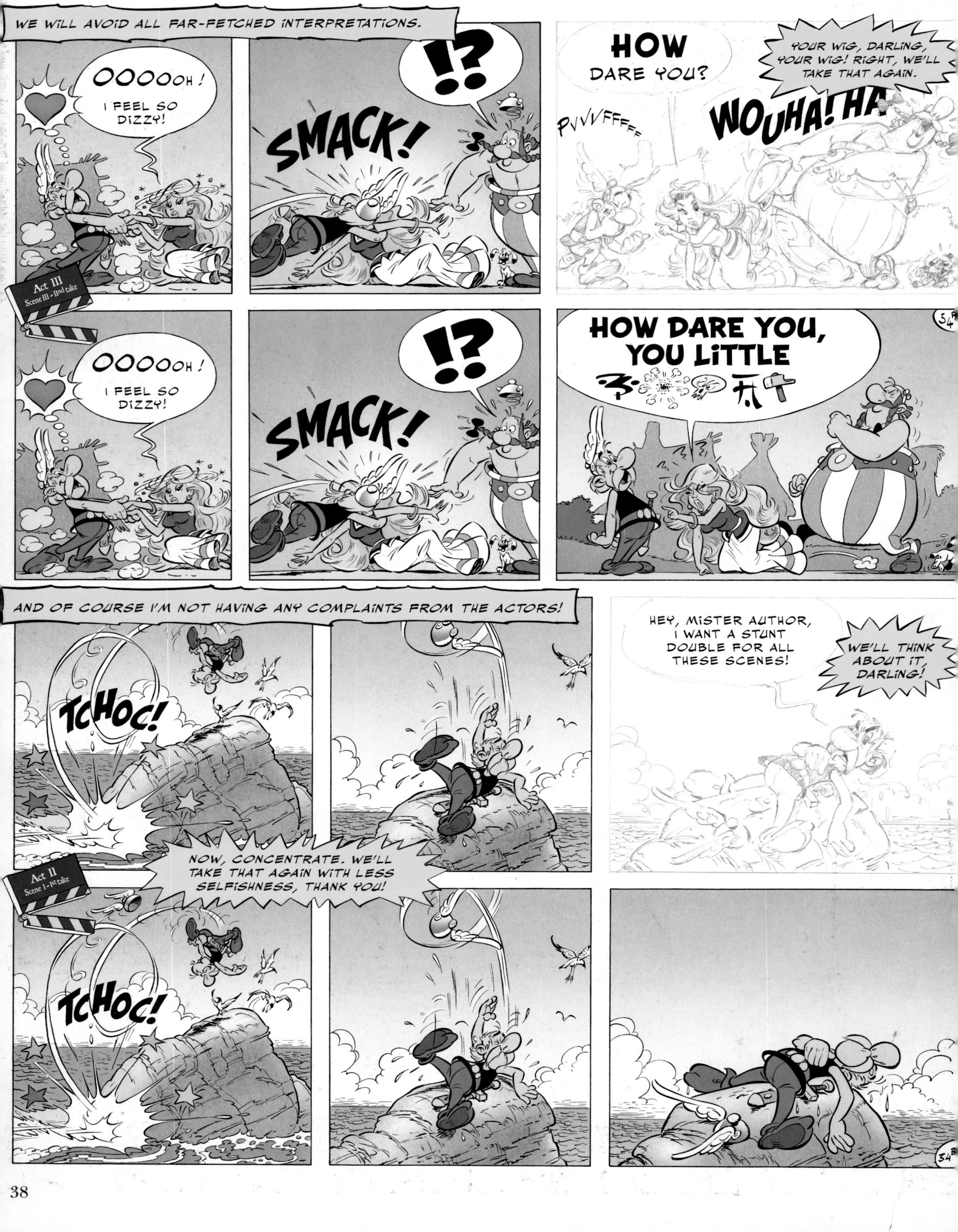
WE WILL AVOID ALL FAR-FETCHED INTERPRETATIONS.
OOOOOH! I FEEL SO DIZZY!
Act III Scene III - IInd take
SMACK!
!?
HOW DARE YOU?
PVVVFFFFF
WOUHA! HA
YOUR WIG, DARLING, YOUR WIG! RIGHT, WE'LL TAKE THAT AGAIN.
OOOOOH! I FEEL SO DIZZY!
SMACK!
!?
HOW DARE YOU, YOU LITTLE
AND OF COURSE I'M NOT HAVING ANY COMPLAINTS FROM THE ACTORS!
TCHOC!
HEY, MISTER AUTHOR, I WANT A STUNT DOUBLE FOR ALL THESE SCENES!
WE'LL THINK ABOUT IT, DARLING!
NOW, CONCENTRATE. WE'LL TAKE THAT AGAIN WITH LESS SELFISHNESS, THANK YOU!
Act II Scene I - 1st take
TCHOC!

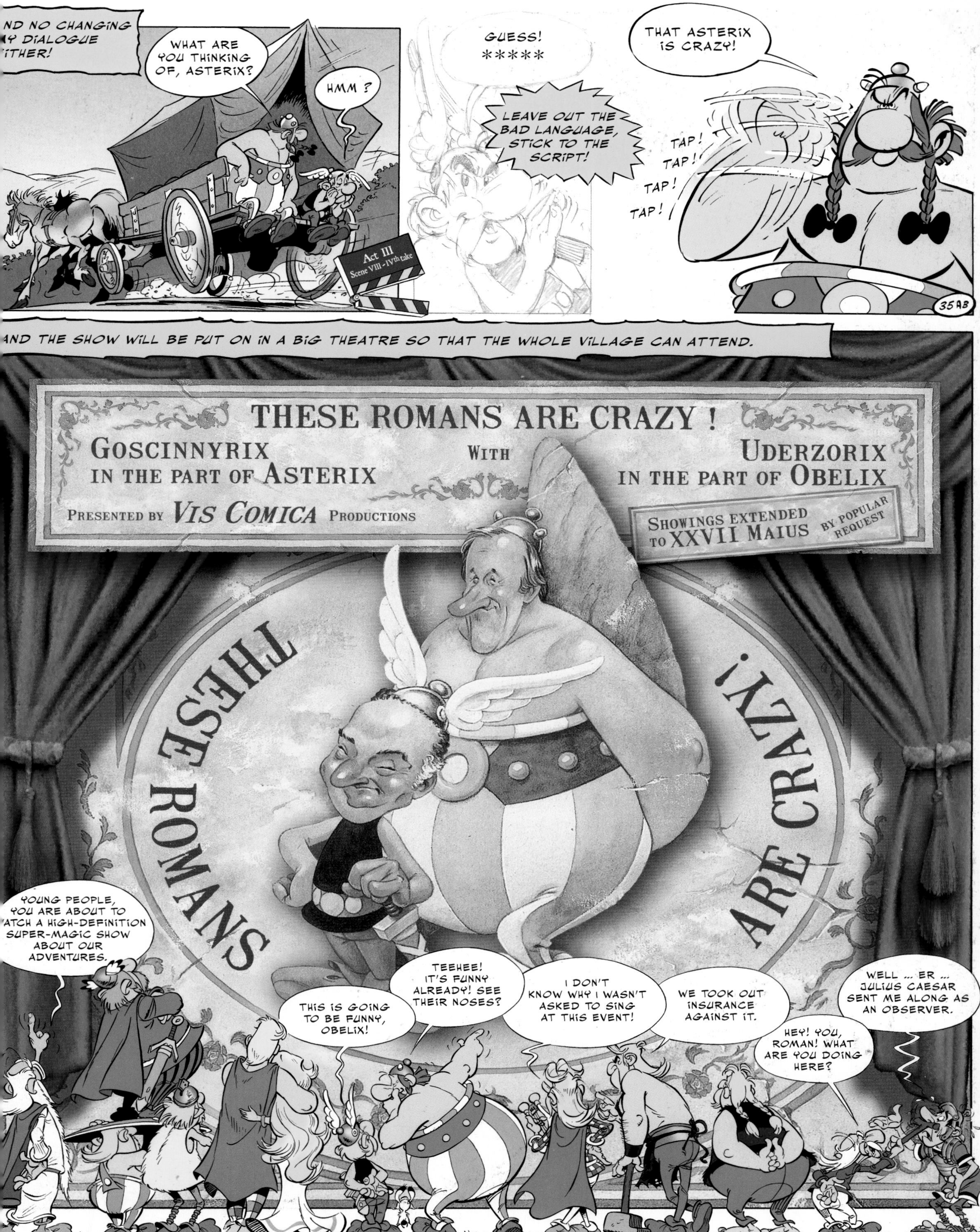
ND NO CHANGING
Y DIALOGUE
ITHER!
WHAT ARE YOU THINKING OF, ASTERIX?
HMM ?
Act III
Scene VIII - IVth take
GUESS! *****
LEAVE OUT THE BAD LANGUAGE, STICK TO THE SCRIPT!
THAT ASTERIX IS CRAZY!
TAP! TAP! TAP! TAP!
35 AB
AND THE SHOW WILL BE PUT ON IN A BIG THEATRE SO THAT THE WHOLE VILLAGE CAN ATTEND.
THESE ROMANS ARE CRAZY !
GOSCINNYRIX IN THE PART OF ASTERIX
WITH
UDERZORIX IN THE PART OF OBELIX
PRESENTED BY VIS COMICA PRODUCTIONS
SHOWINGS EXTENDED TO XXVII MAIUS
BY POPULAR REQUEST
THESE ROMANS ARE CRAZY!
YOUNG PEOPLE, YOU ARE ABOUT TO ATCH A HIGH-DEFINITION SUPER-MAGIC SHOW ABOUT OUR ADVENTURES.
THIS IS GOING TO BE FUNNY, OBELIX!
TEEHEE! IT'S FUNNY ALREADY! SEE THEIR NOSES?
I DON'T KNOW WHY I WASN'T ASKED TO SING AT THIS EVENT!
WE TOOK OUT INSURANCE AGAINST IT.
HEY! YOU, ROMAN! WHAT ARE YOU DOING HERE?
WELL ... ER ... JULIUS CAESAR SENT ME ALONG AS AN OBSERVER.

Frames from the collection of howlers in *Asterix and the Actress*

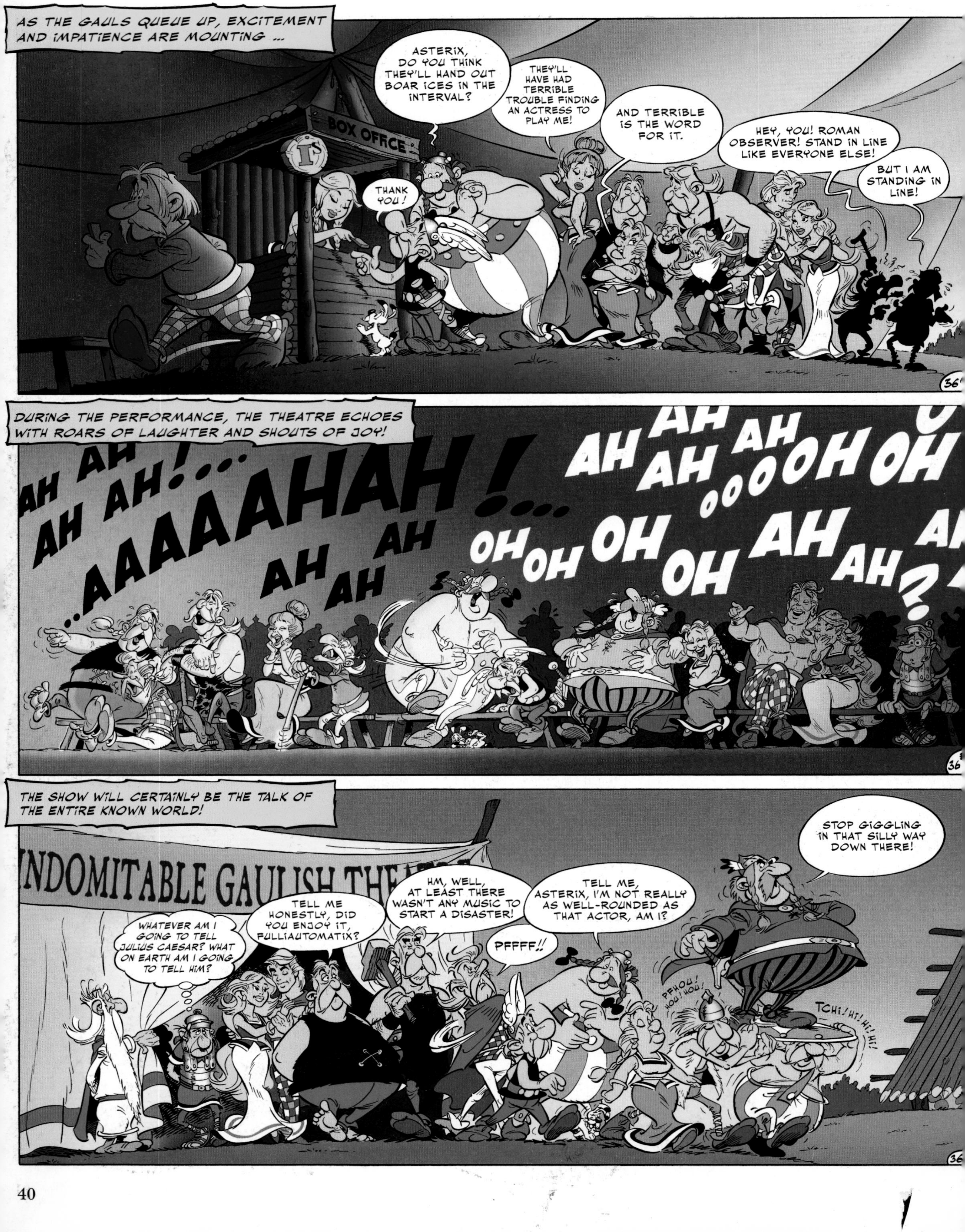
AS THE GAULS QUEUE UP, EXCITEMENT AND IMPATIENCE ARE MOUNTING ...
BOX OFFICE
ASTERIX, DO YOU THINK THEY'LL HAND OUT BOAR ICES IN THE INTERVAL?
THANK YOU!
THEY'LL HAVE HAD TERRIBLE TROUBLE FINDING AN ACTRESS TO PLAY ME!
AND TERRIBLE IS THE WORD FOR IT.
HEY, YOU! ROMAN OBSERVER! STAND IN LINE LIKE EVERYONE ELSE!
BUT I AM STANDING IN LINE!
DURING THE PERFORMANCE, THE THEATRE ECHOES WITH ROARS OF LAUGHTER AND SHOUTS OF JOY!
AH AH AH AH!...
...AAAAAHAH!...
AH AH AH
AH AH AH AH AH OOOOH OH
OH OH OH OH AH AH ?
THE SHOW WILL CERTAINLY BE THE TALK OF THE ENTIRE KNOWN WORLD!
INDOMITABLE GAULISH THEA
WHATEVER AM I GOING TO TELL JULIUS CAESAR? WHAT ON EARTH AM I GOING TO TELL HIM?
TELL ME HONESTLY, DID YOU ENJOY IT, FULLIAUTOMATIX?
HM, WELL, AT LEAST THERE WASN'T ANY MUSIC TO START A DISASTER!
PFFFF!!
TELL ME, ASTERIX, I'M NOT REALLY AS WELL-ROUNDED AS THAT ACTOR, AM I?
STOP GIGGLING IN THAT SILLY WAY DOWN THERE!
PFHOU! HOU! HOU!
TCHI! HI! HI! HI!

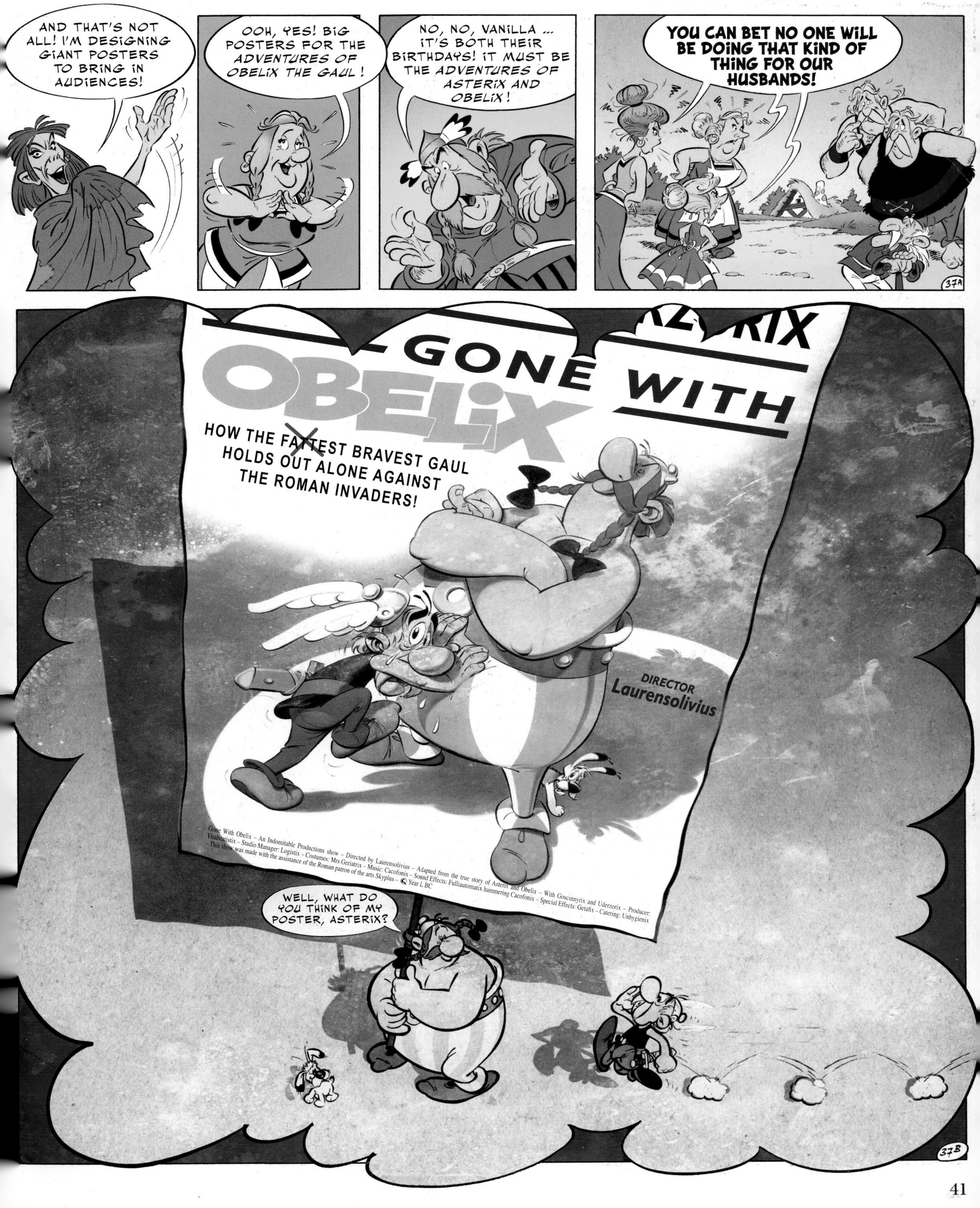
AND THAT'S NOT ALL! I'M DESIGNING GIANT POSTERS TO BRING IN AUDIENCES!
OOH, YES! BIG POSTERS FOR THE ADVENTURES OF OBELIX THE GAUL!
NO, NO, VANILLA ... IT'S BOTH THEIR BIRTHDAYS! IT MUST BE THE ADVENTURES OF ASTERIX AND OBELIX!
YOU CAN BET NO ONE WILL BE DOING THAT KIND OF THING FOR OUR HUSBANDS!
37A
GONE WITH OBELIX
HOW THE FATTEST BRAVEST GAUL HOLDS OUT ALONE AGAINST THE ROMAN INVADERS!
DIRECTOR
Laurensolivius
Gone With Obelix – An Indomitable Productions show – Directed by Laurensolivius – Adapted from the true story of Asterix and Obelix – With Goscinnyrix and Uderzorix – Producer: Vitalstatistix – Studio Manager: Logistix – Costumes: Mrs Geriatrix – Music: Cacofonix – Sound Effects: Fulliautomatix hammering Cacofonix – Special Effects: Getafix – Catering: Unhygienix – This show was made with the assistance of the Roman patron of the arts Skyplus – © Year L BC
WELL, WHAT DO YOU THINK OF MY POSTER, ASTERIX?
37B

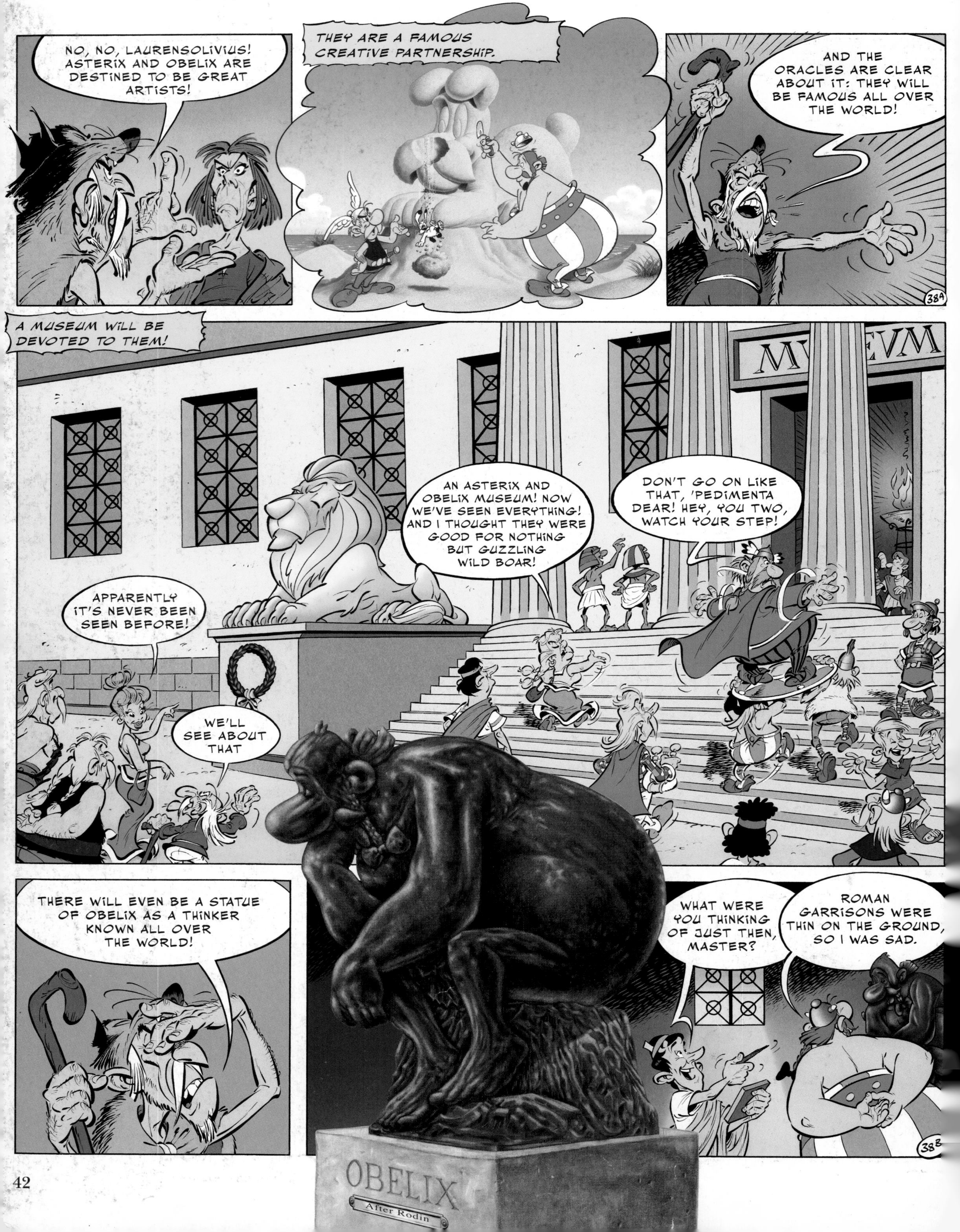
NO, NO, LAURENSOLIVIUS! ASTERIX AND OBELIX ARE DESTINED TO BE GREAT ARTISTS!
THEY ARE A FAMOUS CREATIVE PARTNERSHIP.
AND THE ORACLES ARE CLEAR ABOUT IT: THEY WILL BE FAMOUS ALL OVER THE WORLD!
38A
A MUSEUM WILL BE DEVOTED TO THEM!
MVSEVM
AN ASTERIX AND OBELIX MUSEUM! NOW WE'VE SEEN EVERYTHING! AND I THOUGHT THEY WERE GOOD FOR NOTHING BUT GUZZLING WILD BOAR!
DON'T GO ON LIKE THAT, 'PEDIMENTA DEAR! HEY, YOU TWO, WATCH YOUR STEP!
APPARENTLY IT'S NEVER BEEN SEEN BEFORE!
WE'LL SEE ABOUT THAT
THERE WILL EVEN BE A STATUE OF OBELIX AS A THINKER KNOWN ALL OVER THE WORLD!
WHAT WERE YOU THINKING OF JUST THEN, MASTER?
ROMAN GARRISONS WERE THIN ON THE GROUND, SO I WAS SAD.
38B
OBELIX
After Rodin

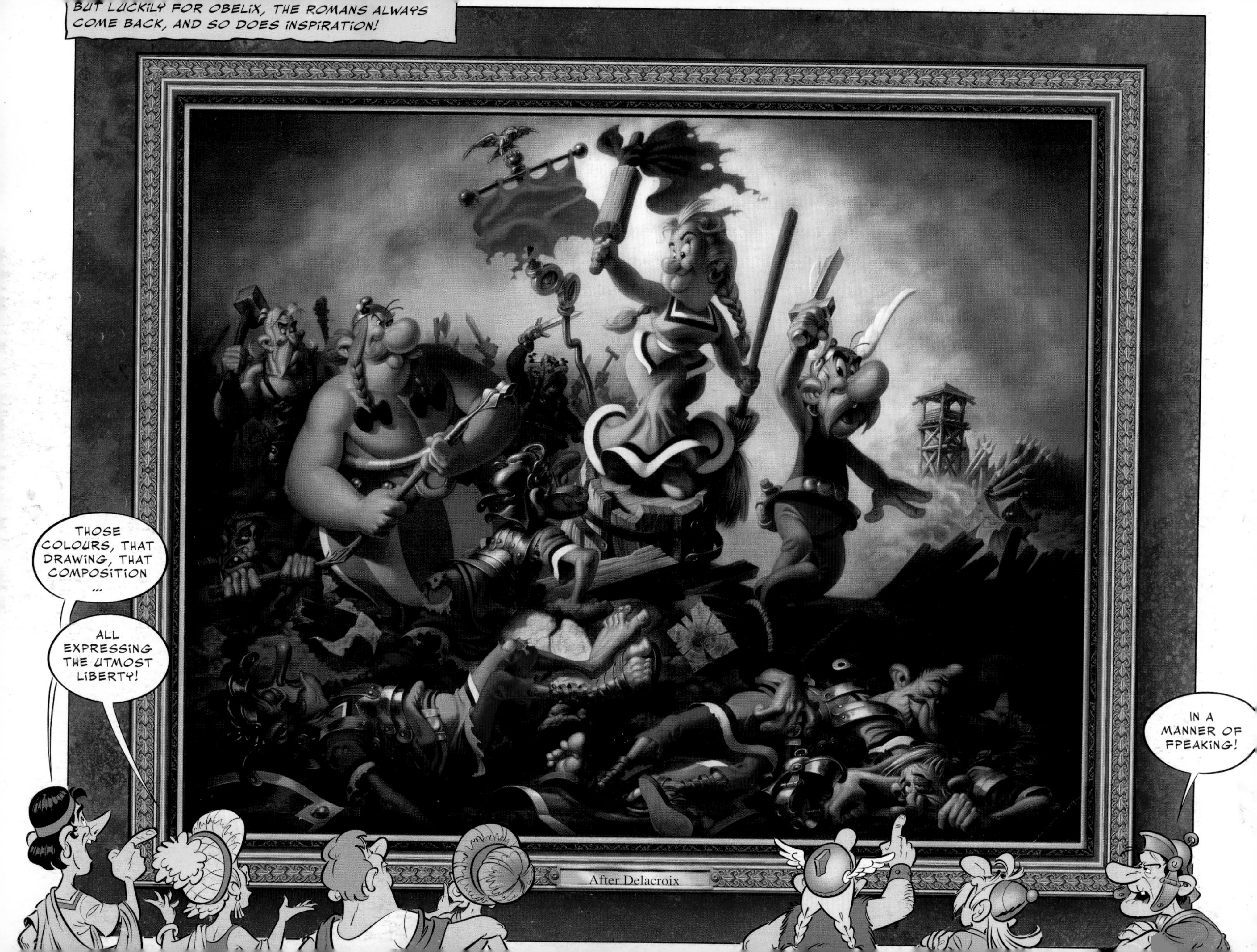
BUT LUCKILY FOR OBELIX, THE ROMANS ALWAYS COME BACK, AND SO DOES INSPIRATION!
THOSE COLOURS, THAT DRAWING, THAT COMPOSITION ...
ALL EXPRESSING THE UTMOST LIBERTY!
After Delacroix
IN A MANNER OF FPEAKING!

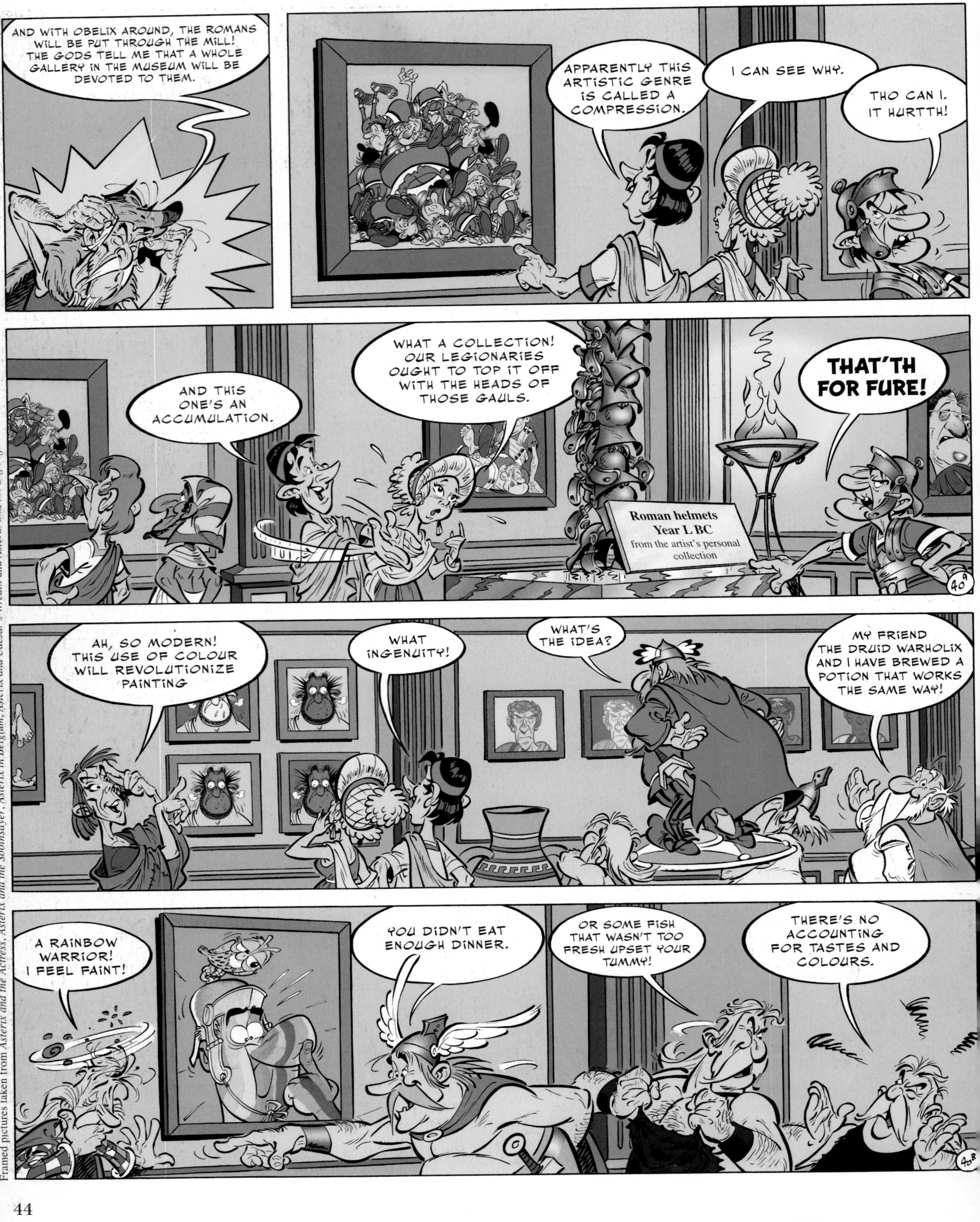

AND WITH OBELIX AROUND, THE ROMANS WILL BE PUT THROUGH THE MILL! THE GODS TELL ME THAT A WHOLE GALLERY IN THE MUSEUM WILL BE DEVOTED TO THEM.
APPARENTLY THIS ARTISTIC GENRE IS CALLED A COMPRESSION.
I CAN SEE WHY.
THO CAN I. IT HURTTH!
AND THIS ONE'S AN ACCUMULATION.
WHAT A COLLECTION! OUR LEGIONARIES OUGHT TO TOP IT OFF WITH THE HEADS OF THOSE GAULS.
Roman helmets
Year L BC
from the artist's personal collection
THAT'TH FOR FURE!
40A
AH, SO MODERN! THIS USE OF COLOUR WILL REVOLUTIONIZE PAINTING
WHAT INGENUITY!
WHAT'S THE IDEA?
MY FRIEND THE DRUID WARHOLIX AND I HAVE BREWED A POTION THAT WORKS THE SAME WAY!
A RAINBOW WARRIOR! I FEEL FAINT!
YOU DIDN'T EAT ENOUGH DINNER.
OR SOME FISH THAT WASN'T TOO FRESH UPSET YOUR TUMMY!
THERE'S NO ACCOUNTING FOR TASTES AND COLOURS.
40B


Framed pictures taken from *Asterix and the Actress*, *Asterix and the Soothsayer*, *Asterix in Belgium*, *Asterix and Caesar's* …

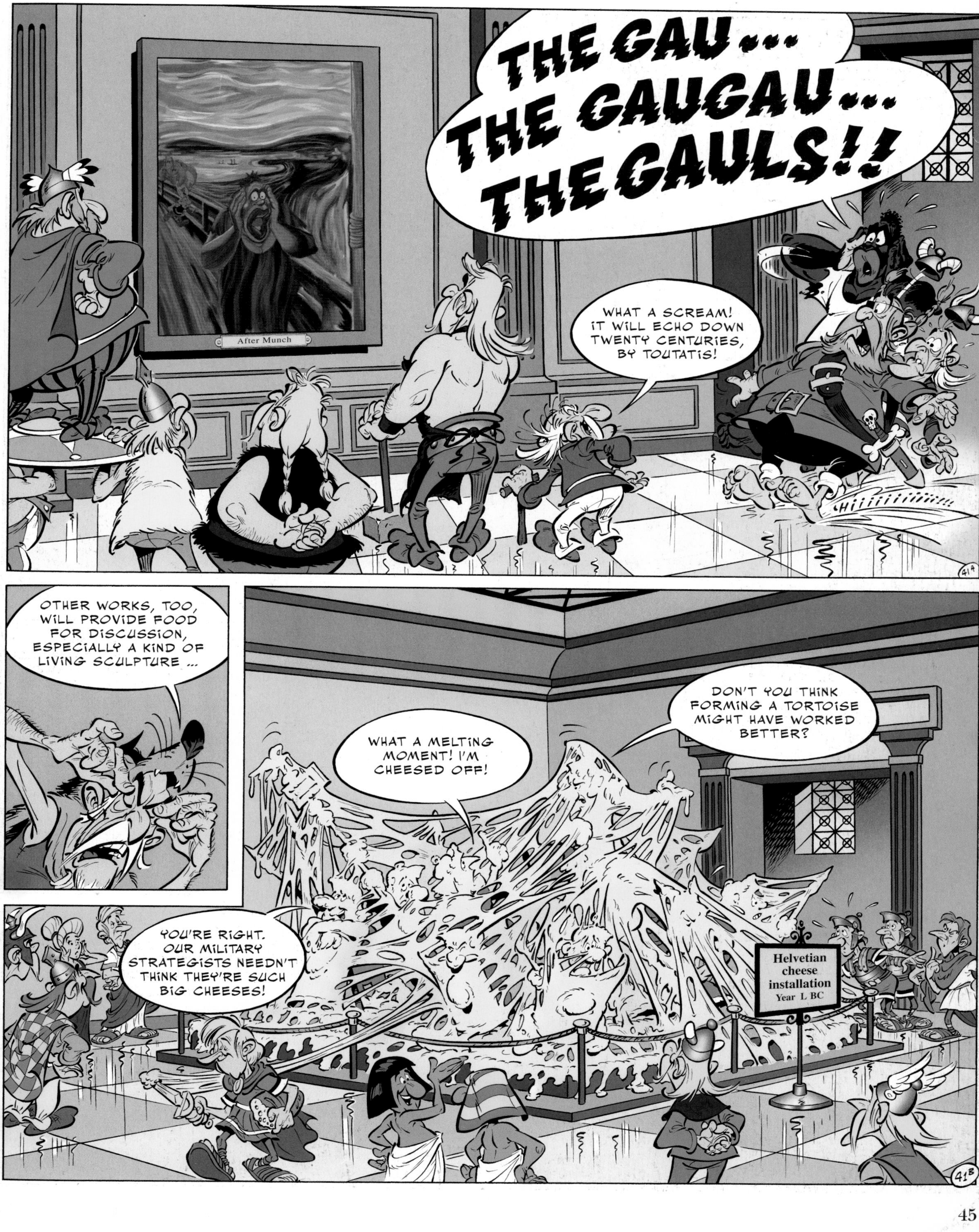
After Munch
THE GAU... THE GAUGAU... THE GAULS!!
WHAT A SCREAM! IT WILL ECHO DOWN TWENTY CENTURIES, BY TOUTATIS!
HIiiiiiiii!!!
OTHER WORKS, TOO, WILL PROVIDE FOOD FOR DISCUSSION, ESPECIALLY A KIND OF LIVING SCULPTURE ...
WHAT A MELTING MOMENT! I'M CHEESED OFF!
DON'T YOU THINK FORMING A TORTOISE MIGHT HAVE WORKED BETTER?
YOU'RE RIGHT. OUR MILITARY STRATEGISTS NEEDN'T THINK THEY'RE SUCH BIG CHEESES!
Helvetian cheese installation Year L BC

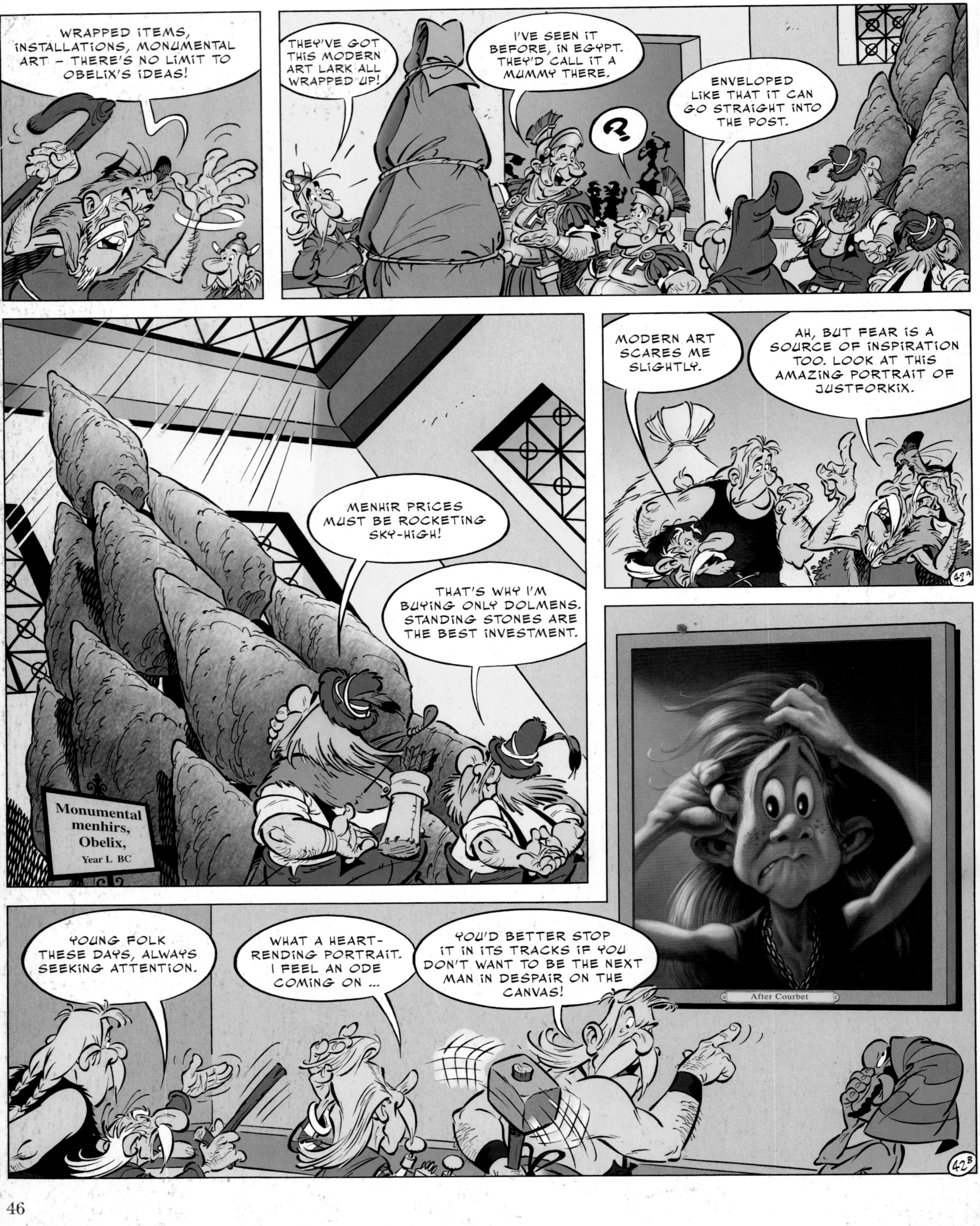

WRAPPED ITEMS, INSTALLATIONS, MONUMENTAL ART – THERE'S NO LIMIT TO OBELIX'S IDEAS!
THEY'VE GOT THIS MODERN ART LARK ALL WRAPPED UP!
I'VE SEEN IT BEFORE, IN EGYPT. THEY'D CALL IT A MUMMY THERE.
?
ENVELOPED LIKE THAT IT CAN GO STRAIGHT INTO THE POST.
MENHIR PRICES MUST BE ROCKETING SKY-HIGH!
THAT'S WHY I'M BUYING ONLY DOLMENS. STANDING STONES ARE THE BEST INVESTMENT.
Monumental menhirs, Obelix, Year L BC
MODERN ART SCARES ME SLIGHTLY.
AH, BUT FEAR IS A SOURCE OF INSPIRATION TOO. LOOK AT THIS AMAZING PORTRAIT OF JUSTFORKIX.
42A
After Courbet
YOUNG FOLK THESE DAYS, ALWAYS SEEKING ATTENTION.
WHAT A HEART-RENDING PORTRAIT. I FEEL AN ODE COMING ON ...
YOU'D BETTER STOP IT IN ITS TRACKS IF YOU DON'T WANT TO BE THE NEXT MAN IN DESPAIR ON THE CANVAS!
42B

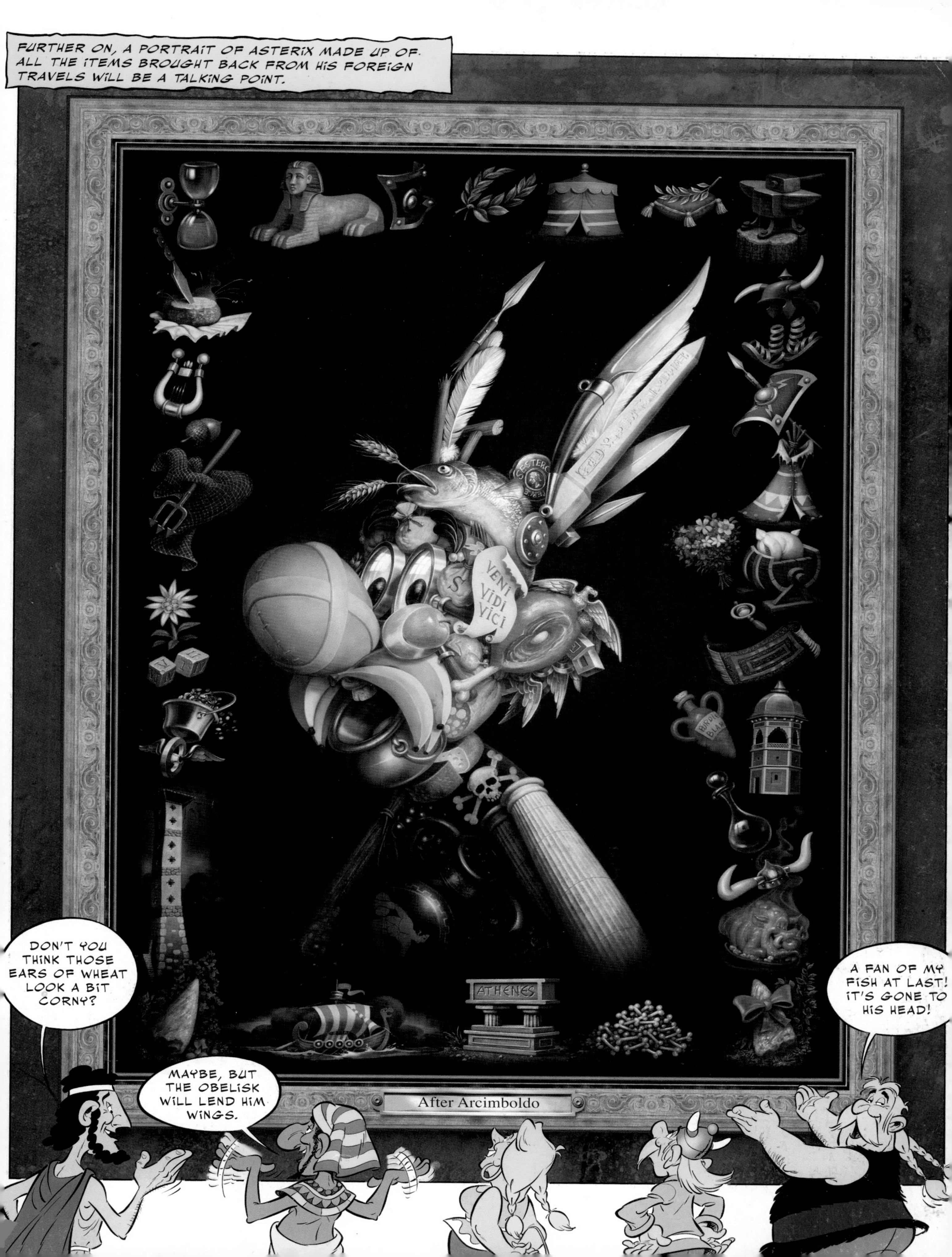
FURTHER ON, A PORTRAIT OF ASTERIX MADE UP OF ALL THE ITEMS BROUGHT BACK FROM HIS FOREIGN TRAVELS WILL BE A TALKING POINT.
VENI VIDI VICI
ATHENES
After Arcimboldo
DON'T YOU THINK THOSE EARS OF WHEAT LOOK A BIT CORNY?
MAYBE, BUT THE OBELISK WILL LEND HIM WINGS.
A FAN OF MY FISH AT LAST! IT'S GONE TO HIS HEAD!

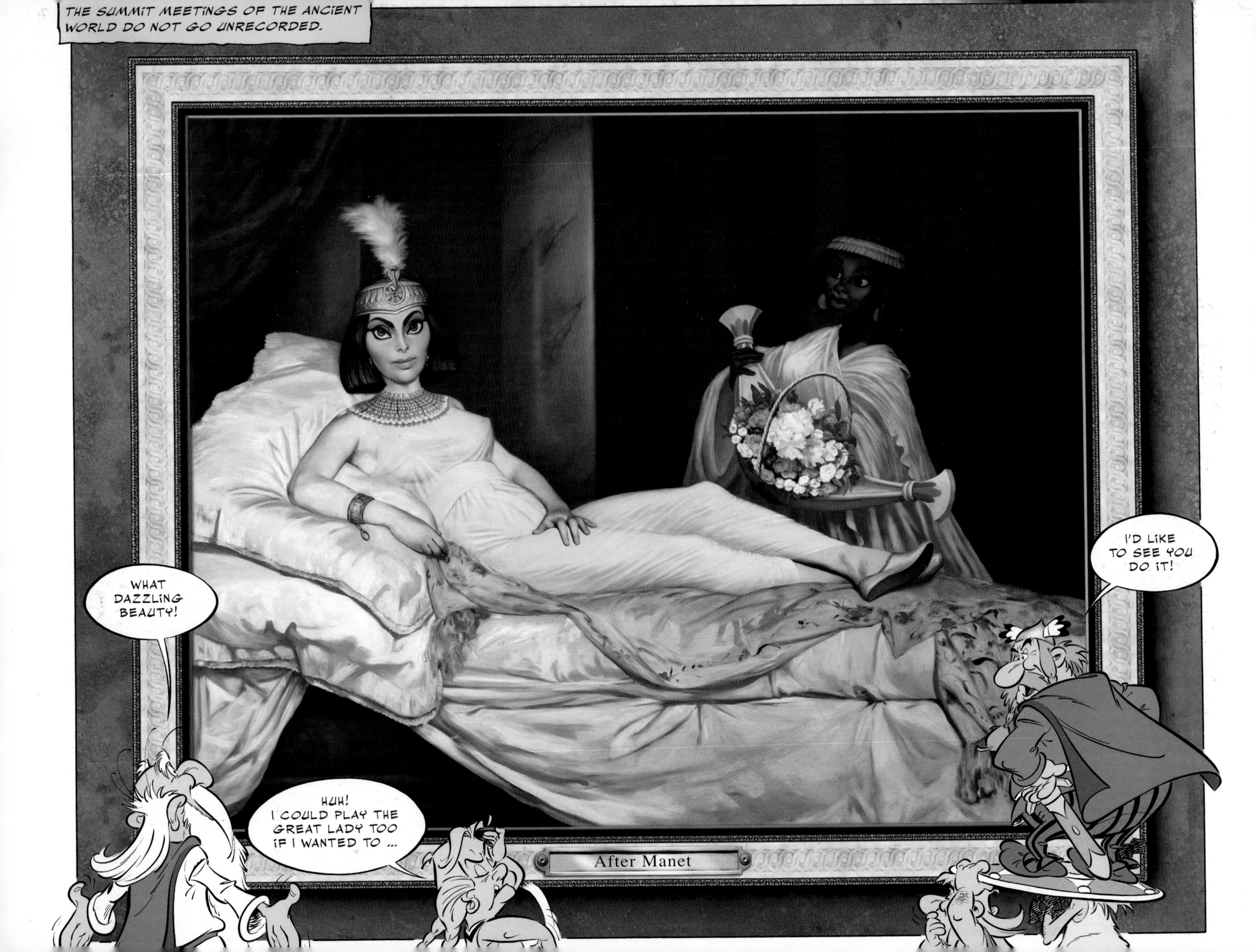
THE SUMMIT MEETINGS OF THE ANCIENT WORLD DO NOT GO UNRECORDED.
After Manet
WHAT DAZZLING BEAUTY!
HUH! I COULD PLAY THE GREAT LADY TOO IF I WANTED TO ...
I'D LIKE TO SEE YOU DO IT!

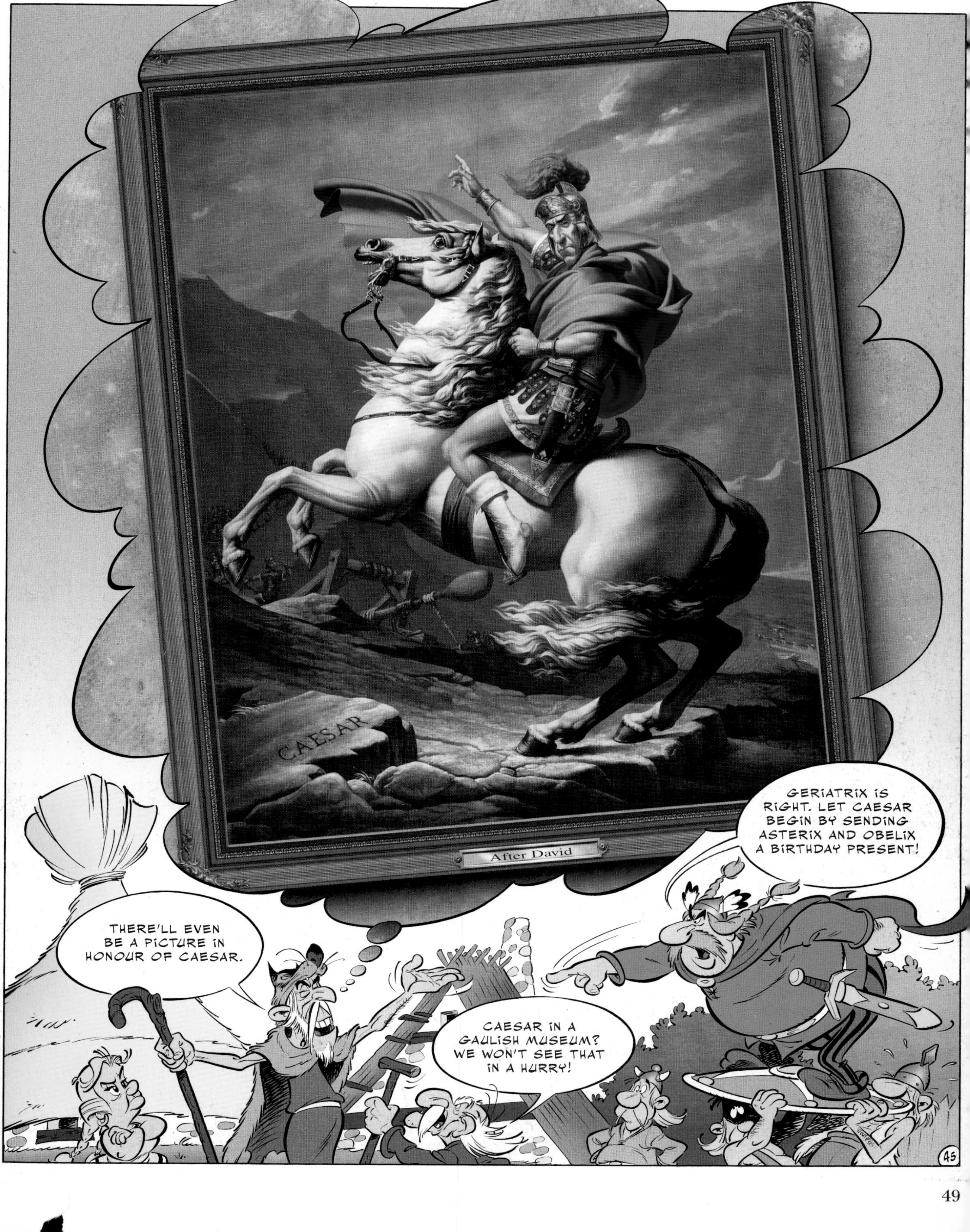
CAESAR
After David
THERE'LL EVEN BE A PICTURE IN HONOUR OF CAESAR.
GERIATRIX IS RIGHT. LET CAESAR BEGIN BY SENDING ASTERIX AND OBELIX A BIRTHDAY PRESENT!
CAESAR IN A GAULISH MUSEUM? WE WON'T SEE THAT IN A HURRY!
45

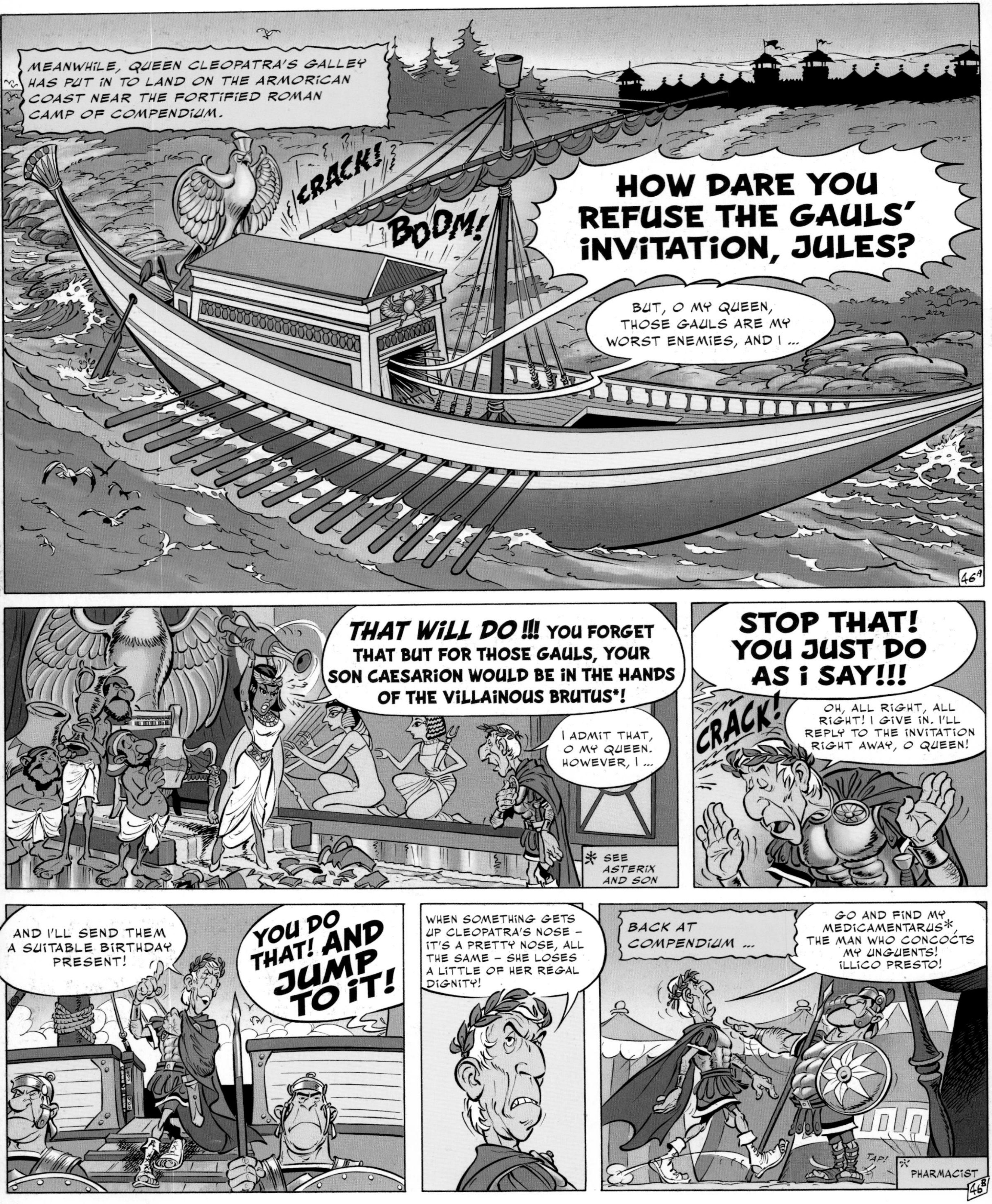
MEANWHILE, QUEEN CLEOPATRA'S GALLEY HAS PUT IN TO LAND ON THE ARMORICAN COAST NEAR THE FORTIFIED ROMAN CAMP OF COMPENDIUM.
CRACK!
BOOM!
HOW DARE YOU REFUSE THE GAULS' INVITATION, JULES?
BUT, O MY QUEEN, THOSE GAULS ARE MY WORST ENEMIES, AND I ...
46A
THAT WILL DO !!! YOU FORGET THAT BUT FOR THOSE GAULS, YOUR SON CAESARION WOULD BE IN THE HANDS OF THE VILLAINOUS BRUTUS*!
I ADMIT THAT, O MY QUEEN. HOWEVER, I ...
* SEE ASTERIX AND SON
STOP THAT! YOU JUST DO AS I SAY!!!
CRACK!
OH, ALL RIGHT, ALL RIGHT! I GIVE IN. I'LL REPLY TO THE INVITATION RIGHT AWAY, O QUEEN!
AND I'LL SEND THEM A SUITABLE BIRTHDAY PRESENT!
YOU DO THAT! AND JUMP TO IT!
WHEN SOMETHING GETS UP CLEOPATRA'S NOSE – IT'S A PRETTY NOSE, ALL THE SAME – SHE LOSES A LITTLE OF HER REGAL DIGNITY!
BACK AT COMPENDIUM ...
GO AND FIND MY MEDICAMENTARUS*, THE MAN WHO CONCOCTS MY UNGUENTS! ILLICO PRESTO!
TAP!
* PHARMACIST
46B

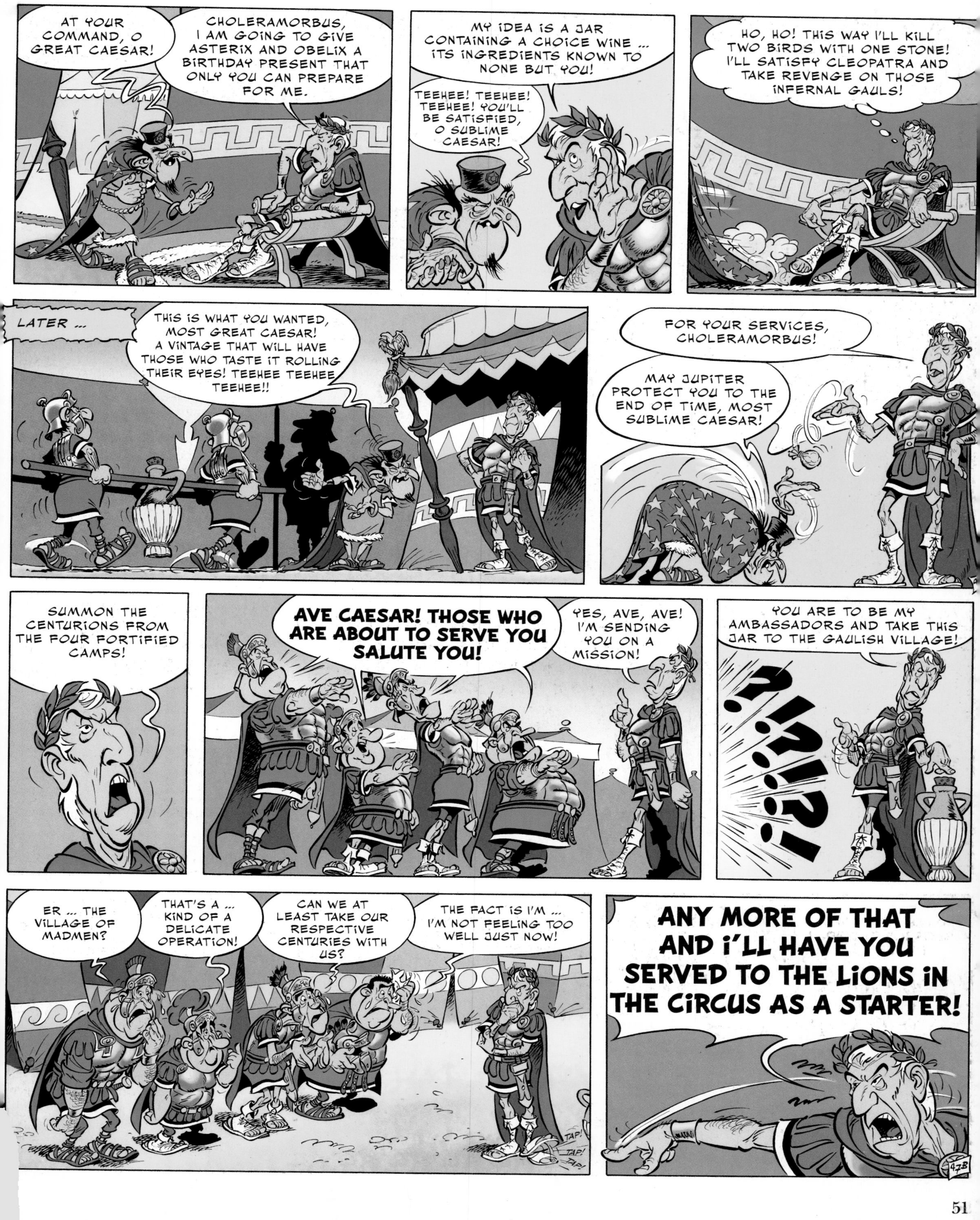
AT YOUR COMMAND, O GREAT CAESAR!
CHOLERAMORBUS, I AM GOING TO GIVE ASTERIX AND OBELIX A BIRTHDAY PRESENT THAT ONLY YOU CAN PREPARE FOR ME.
MY IDEA IS A JAR CONTAINING A CHOICE WINE ... ITS INGREDIENTS KNOWN TO NONE BUT YOU!
TEEHEE! TEEHEE! TEEHEE! YOU'LL BE SATISFIED, O SUBLIME CAESAR!
HO, HO! THIS WAY I'LL KILL TWO BIRDS WITH ONE STONE! I'LL SATISFY CLEOPATRA AND TAKE REVENGE ON THOSE INFERNAL GAULS!
LATER ...
THIS IS WHAT YOU WANTED, MOST GREAT CAESAR! A VINTAGE THAT WILL HAVE THOSE WHO TASTE IT ROLLING THEIR EYES! TEEHEE TEEHEE TEEHEE!!
FOR YOUR SERVICES, CHOLERAMORBUS!
MAY JUPITER PROTECT YOU TO THE END OF TIME, MOST SUBLIME CAESAR!
SUMMON THE CENTURIONS FROM THE FOUR FORTIFIED CAMPS!
AVE CAESAR! THOSE WHO ARE ABOUT TO SERVE YOU SALUTE YOU!
YES, AVE, AVE! I'M SENDING YOU ON A MISSION!
YOU ARE TO BE MY AMBASSADORS AND TAKE THIS JAR TO THE GAULISH VILLAGE!
?!?!?!
ER ... THE VILLAGE OF MADMEN?
THAT'S A ... KIND OF A DELICATE OPERATION!
CAN WE AT LEAST TAKE OUR RESPECTIVE CENTURIES WITH US?
THE FACT IS I'M ... I'M NOT FEELING TOO WELL JUST NOW!
TAP! TAP! TAP!
ANY MORE OF THAT AND I'LL HAVE YOU SERVED TO THE LIONS IN THE CIRCUS AS A STARTER!

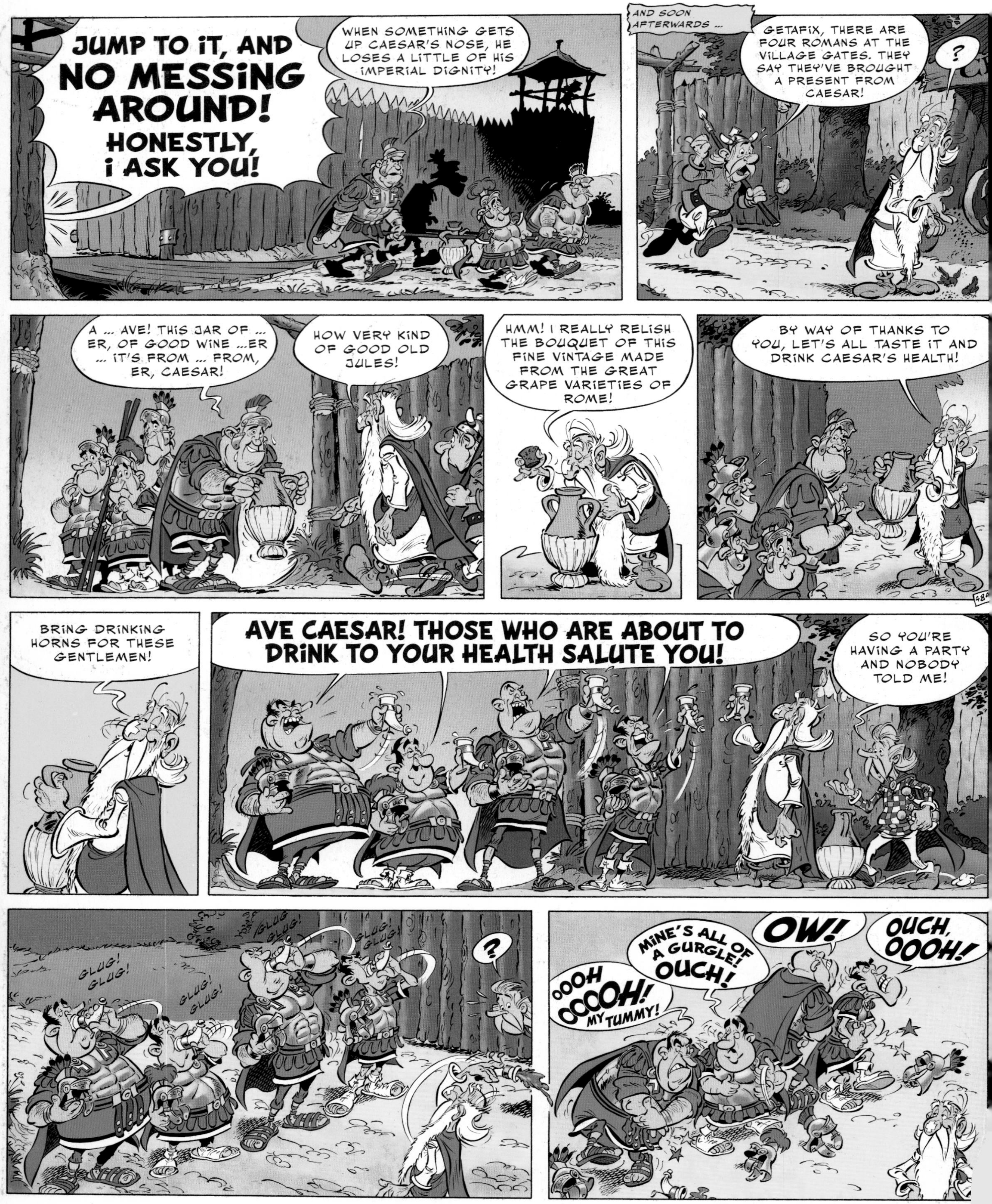
JUMP TO IT, AND NO MESSING AROUND! HONESTLY, I ASK YOU!
WHEN SOMETHING GETS UP CAESAR'S NOSE, HE LOSES A LITTLE OF HIS IMPERIAL DIGNITY!
AND SOON AFTERWARDS ...
GETAFIX, THERE ARE FOUR ROMANS AT THE VILLAGE GATES. THEY SAY THEY'VE BROUGHT A PRESENT FROM CAESAR!
?
A ... AVE! THIS JAR OF ... ER, OF GOOD WINE ...ER ... IT'S FROM ... FROM, ER, CAESAR!
HOW VERY KIND OF GOOD OLD JULES!
HMM! I REALLY RELISH THE BOUQUET OF THIS FINE VINTAGE MADE FROM THE GREAT GRAPE VARIETIES OF ROME!
BY WAY OF THANKS TO YOU, LET'S ALL TASTE IT AND DRINK CAESAR'S HEALTH!
BRING DRINKING HORNS FOR THESE GENTLEMEN!
AVE CAESAR! THOSE WHO ARE ABOUT TO DRINK TO YOUR HEALTH SALUTE YOU!
SO YOU'RE HAVING A PARTY AND NOBODY TOLD ME!
GLUG! GLUG!
GLUG! GLUG!
GLUG! GLUG!
GLUG! GLUG!
?
OOOH OOOOH! MY TUMMY!
MINE'S ALL OF A GURGLE! OUCH!
OW!
OUCH, OOOH!

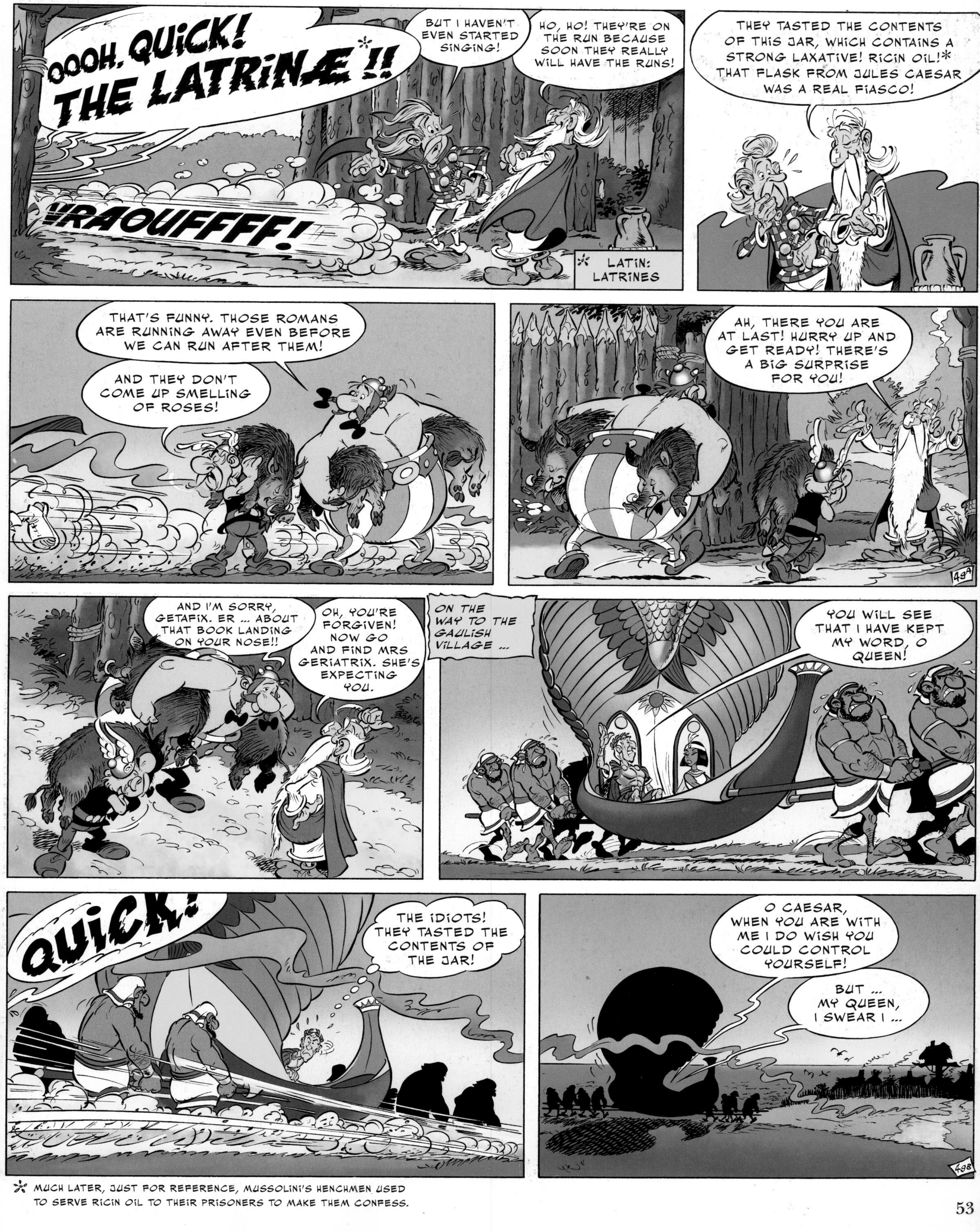
OOOH, QUICK! THE LATRINÆ !!*
BUT I HAVEN'T EVEN STARTED SINGING!
HO, HO! THEY'RE ON THE RUN BECAUSE SOON THEY REALLY WILL HAVE THE RUNS!
VRAOUFFFF!
* LATIN: LATRINES
THEY TASTED THE CONTENTS OF THIS JAR, WHICH CONTAINS A STRONG LAXATIVE! RICIN OIL!* THAT FLASK FROM JULES CAESAR WAS A REAL FIASCO!
THAT'S FUNNY. THOSE ROMANS ARE RUNNING AWAY EVEN BEFORE WE CAN RUN AFTER THEM!
AND THEY DON'T COME UP SMELLING OF ROSES!
AH, THERE YOU ARE AT LAST! HURRY UP AND GET READY! THERE'S A BIG SURPRISE FOR YOU!
AND I'M SORRY, GETAFIX. ER ... ABOUT THAT BOOK LANDING ON YOUR NOSE!!
OH, YOU'RE FORGIVEN! NOW GO AND FIND MRS GERIATRIX. SHE'S EXPECTING YOU.
ON THE WAY TO THE GAULISH VILLAGE ...
YOU WILL SEE THAT I HAVE KEPT MY WORD, O QUEEN!
QUICK!
THE IDIOTS! THEY TASTED THE CONTENTS OF THE JAR!
O CAESAR, WHEN YOU ARE WITH ME I DO WISH YOU COULD CONTROL YOURSELF!
BUT ... MY QUEEN, I SWEAR I ...

* MUCH LATER, JUST FOR REFERENCE, MUSSOLINI'S HENCHMEN USED TO SERVE RICIN OIL TO THEIR PRISONERS TO MAKE THEM CONFESS.

*At last all our friends are reunited in the village square, and the guests give the birthday boys a lovely surprise.*

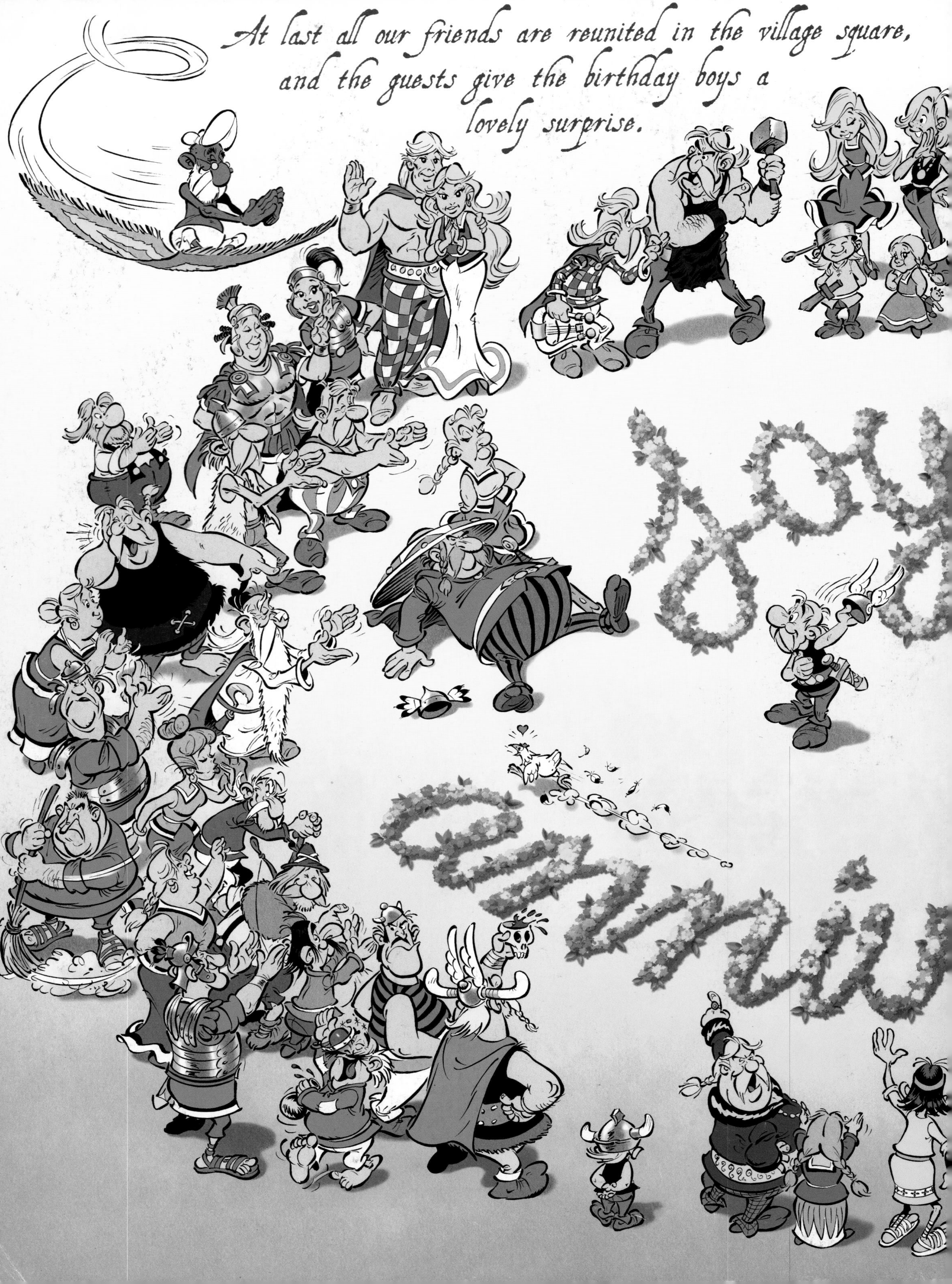

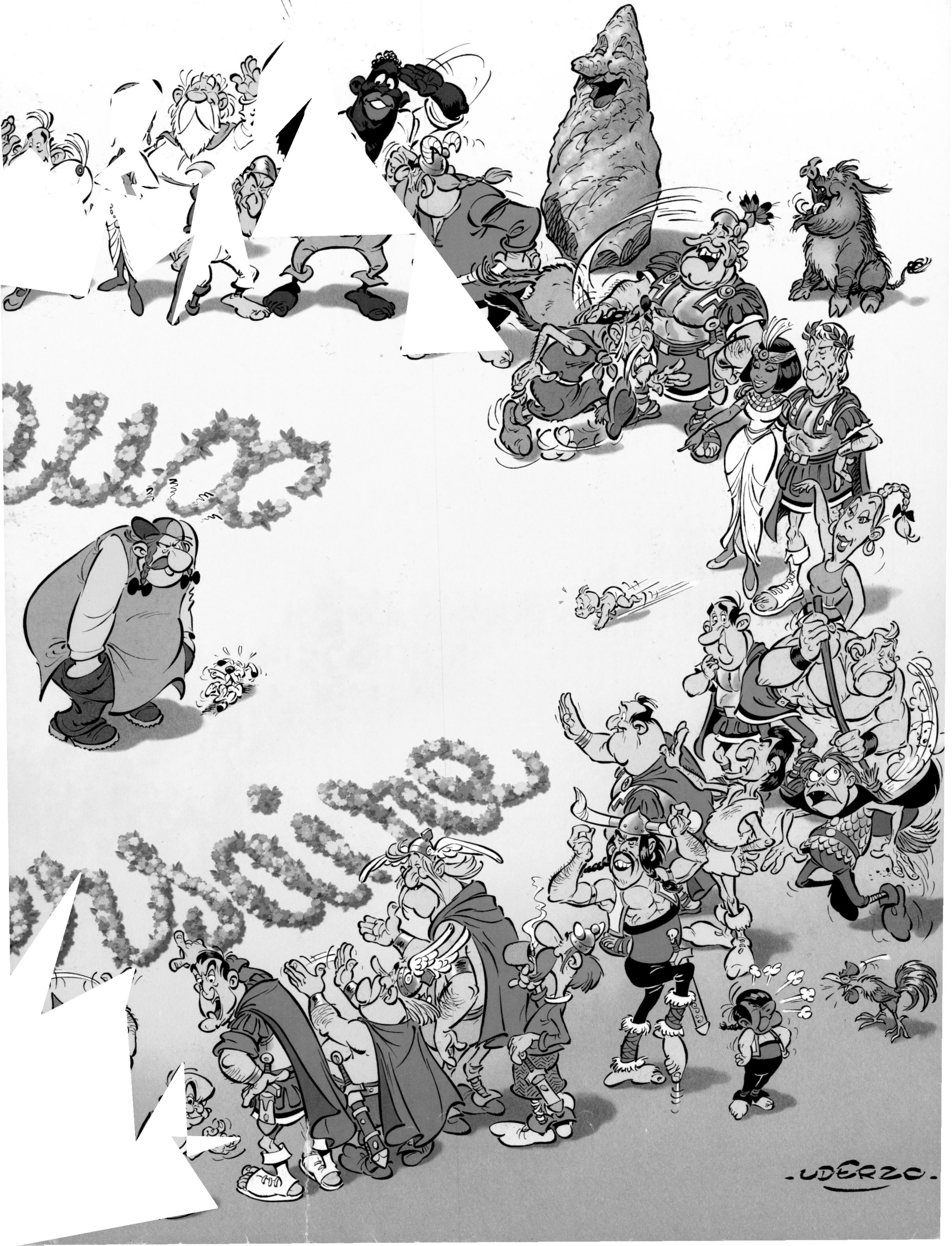
-UDERZO-

I would like to mention all those who have contributed their talents to producing this album:

**Régis GRÉBENT**, head of Studio 56, and his entire team.
**Frédéric** et **Thierry MÉBARKI**, two remarkably talented brothers.
**Dionen CLAUTEAUX**, son of the man who first had the idea for the magazine *PILOTE*.
And all the people – too many for me to mention everyone by name – who believed in this *GOLDEN BOOK*.

Albert UDERZO

✽ ✽ ✽ ✽ ✽ ✽

Original title: *L'ANNIVERSAIRE D'ASTÉRIX ET OBÉLIX: Le Livre D'or*

Original edition © 2009 Les Éditions Albert René/Goscinny-Uderzo
English translation © 2009 Les Éditions Albert René/Goscinny-Uderzo

Exclusive licensee: Orion Publishing Group
Translator: Anthea Bell
Typography: Bryony Newhouse

This edition first published in 2010 by Orion Books Ltd, Orion House, 5 Upper St Martin's Lane, London WC2H 9EA. An Hachette UK company.

1 3 5 7 9 10 8 6 4 2

Printed in China.

The Orion Publishing Group's policy is to use papers that are natural, renewable and recyclable and made from wood grown in sustainable forests. The logging and manufacturing processes are expected to conform to the environmental regulations of the country of origin.

A CIP Catalogue record for this book is available from the British Library

ISBN 978-1-4440-0095-5

www.orionbooks.co.uk

www.asterix.com/english/